DOGZ
a novel

Tom Bacchus

also by Tom Bacchus

BONE
RAHM
POKE
Q-FAQ
Doin' the Town, a naughty nautical novella

Copyright 2024. Tom Bacchus.

This is a work of fiction. Names, characters, places, and incidents either are the product of the author's imagination or are used fictitiously, and any resemblance to actual persons, living or dead, business establishments, events, or locales is entirely coincidental.

All rights reserved. No part of this book may be reproduced in any form or by any means without prior written consent of the Publisher, excepting brief quotes used in reviews, or after sexual favors have been provided.

Cover photo & design: Tom Bacchus

Library of Congress Catalog #TK

Bacchus, Tom 1969–
DOGZ, a novel

ISBN print: 9798218447038
Ebook: 9798218447045

1. Fiction 2. Gay Fiction 3. Literary Fiction 4. 1990s 5. San Francisco 6. Erotica 7. Sexuality 10. Homosexuality

"Love comes slyly, like a thief."

– Jean Genet

1

I like to think that writing helps one forget. Once I've put memories down, poured them into a computer, sold them, had them printed on thousands of copies, seen them in the hands of men in bookstores, known that they lay beside their beds on a lonely night, I like to think that I can begin to forget.

Of course I'm wrong. I am cursed with total recall.

Every click of the keyboard burns him back into me, and every printed copy, going who knows where, only spreads the virus that was him. Every spurt of your come, and thousands of others, spawns his demonic joy onto the dream-wracked bedsheets of a nation of lonely queers. He is the Patient Zero of broken passions.

But who am I to criticize.

I called him Griffin the Second, an unusual name for two very different men. My first Griffin was a well-mannered corporate executive I met in a straight bar, of all places. He was short and balding, but muscular and immensely handsome, with a missile of cock. It looked great sticking straight out of his business suit in the morning when I blew him after breakfast. He liked that.

I called him Little Big Man. He didn't like that.

But that's several years and three thousand miles ago. It was the year of Griffin the Second. A year of passion, pain, emptiness and regret.

I was considering it all again, in a moment of indecision. I sat on the toilet, having taken a good dump. My pipe was missing, my papers mythic in their disappearance. I was going to stuff the end with the last shreds of pot left on the folded crease of a Cock Factory flyer for Wet Night.

I felt good, though, despite my poverty, for it was the sort of poverty that still left me fed, entertained and occasionally altered.

I smoked, wiped and swayed around my apartment, pants unbuckled, cock out, listening to Gregorian chants and Steve Reich's "Drumming."

One of the strange flaws of my dual cassette boom box is the ability to play two sounds at once. I kept forgetting to get a mixer and capture these hybrids. I also couldn't afford one, what with all the repairs and loan payoffs on Rose, my Honda, but that usually didn't stop my occasional splurges.

I should have been sad, having walked to the Safeway at midnight on a Friday to buy what my dateless gut craved - an entire peach pie. The five blocks seemed too short to get the motorcycle I call Rose out of the garage, and besides, I always missed so much under that helmet. I was almost ready to face men again.

I could have been comforted by the sight of dozens of other equally sullen attractive young men caught at midnight, like me, without a date, splurging on Cadbury chocolate bars, pork chops, or tabloids, guilty as a police line-up in the Ten Items or Less aisle.

But what sent me into a warm wave of comfortable relief under the half moonlight and the glare of the Mint (the real mint, the monolith above the Safeway, not the gay bar) was the sight I witnessed coming home, passing an intersection outside the market, the plastic bags weighing down each of my hands. The late night buses only passed fitfully on weekend nights.

Through a serene act of timing thanks to the gods of lost love, or perhaps the fact that I spent an extra minute in the bakery section, I saw a bus pass the moment I approached the intersection. On the bus, yawning under the hideous fluorescent light, sporting a pathetically cheerful new hair color and obviously headed to some desperate club for alcoholic fun, was Griffin the Second.

It pleased me, not to see such downfall, but that a bit of simple tedium had once again entered his life as well, after all those fireworks. I felt real, clear, warm and utterly equal.

Back home, I ate a slice of the pie, then felt better and decided to go out. Maybe it was because I knew where Griffin was headed, and every other direction seemed safe.

If it weren't for the sliver of desire to turn and catch that bus.

2

The first second I saw him, I knew I was in trouble. Harlan's warning didn't help.

This was only a week after I'd temporarily moved to San Francisco. Harlan had preceded me by a few years from New York City, and set me up with the interview for a year-long job creating a new gay magazine.

This was after years of freelancing and then finally getting a job in Toronto to help start a magazine there. I was paid generously, spending most of it with lap dances at the strip club Remington's. I lost count of all the Canadian uncut stripper cocks I had wagging in my face.

So with that and a few other job references, Harlan finagled me getting this job, and a tip on a cheap apartment (and a profitable illegal sublet of my East Village boite), allowing me to get paid to enjoy San Francisco for the first time.

Oh, a note I should add. Years after all this, when was it? 2019, before the plague? I returned to San Francisco for Folsom Week and a design. Conference; how convenient. Just to stroll literally down memory lane, I checked out the apartment that I'd rented that year and a half in 1993-4ish.

Colorful planters out front, a new paint job, a 'Sold' sign. I couldn't peek upstairs, but it looked like it had been renovated, properly staged to remove any scent of previous tenants, myself included. I looked it up on Zillow; going for like a million-three.

I suppose if I were more poetic, I would've put this in as an epilogue, but I just thought of it now while I was here on this page, so fuck it.

Back to our story.

This was back in the days when there were nightclubs worth going to in San Francisco, when you could strike up a conversation with a guy without a sardonic glance, that with a bit of booze and the thud of a disco beat, or in this case, Nine Inch Nails, since it was Paula's Clubhouse, now closed, a haven of alternative post-punk neo-goth amusement, one could find a friend or a fuck for the night, or the moment, or just enjoy the scene and the music and feel good.

I remember that always, the thud of Nine Inch Nails' "Down In It," and my feet tapping out the insistent guilt-ridden industrial beat.

I was midway through gritting out a lyric or two, when my friend Harlan, whom I had long since given up flirting with or trying to tease into friendly bedroom situations, started a moment and said the words that changed my year forever.

"Oh, there's Griffin."

We were sitting at a table, sipping beers and babbling about the videos, the music and the crowd. Walking up to us was the embodiment of all that the costumed crowd of queers strove to be. Dressed down, funky, yet glaringly sexual, Griffin had all that and more.

He met Harlan's eyes, but lingered only a moment, as if seeing Harlan for what he was, an insufferably cute man, but a discarded conquest, while I was fresh, and Harlan the passage to me.

Harlan introduced us, and we shook hands. Griffin's smile betrayed an evil joy, like a kid who smashed windows just for the sound of it.

1970s porn sub with the early '90s post-punk arrogance of the time; at first, I thought his eyes were green, but then it might've been the bar lighting, a flick of yellow somewhere, one of several details among his incredibly handsome qualities that didn't sink in until after he's left the room.

Griffin was just my height, with short brown hair in a stylish punky cut, short on the sides, with a slat of hair flipped over on one side. He had earrings in each side, a black T-shirt, and baggy white jeans rolled up a bit to show off his worn Doc Martins. I imagined some body part I couldn't see was pierced. It was casually hip dress, and underneath I could tell his body with like mine, thin, yet toned with a bit of muscle. Boyish, nothing amazing, but that smile and those eyes. They glimmered with nasty possibilities.

I forget the next intoxicated minutes. We ended up strolling together through the club's tiny space, awaiting a performance by Pansy Cray-Cray, resident pop drag icon of the year, and unlike me, on her way up.

Harlan was off chatting with a handsome fellow of questionable breeding. Griffin and I began chatting about cultural stupidities, and our casual remove from the scene. His laughter was hearty and loud for such a small guy, like myself.

"You know, you oughtta be in my zine," I said impulsively, knowing what I might be getting myself into.

"You've gotta be crazy."

"No, I'm serious."

"Okay, what's it called?"

"DOGZ. For men who need to be on a leash."

"Dogs! I love it! Awhoooo!" He howled above the music. People turned and stared. He didn't mind at all. Neither did I.

I told him about DOGZ and how I started it by just copy-pasting a bunch of silly naked images and text in my kitchen and then giving them away Pyramid Club and other places until they started asking for more. I started making multiple copies, selling them and shipping them around the country. I stopped after a bit because the music was loud and I was shouting and didn't even think he was paying attention.

We drank, and danced, and it took him about a minute to get in close and dance with me. I still had the beer bottle in my hand, and felt awkward. It didn't help when the bottle foamed up and spilled out over my cold fingers and onto the floor.

"A bit premature," he joked.

"I usually hold out pretty good," I said.

"Gotta have a real need," he grinned. "Do you need it?"

We traded numbers and agreed to meet up in a few days to talk about a possible photo shoot for my fledgling zine.

After a bit more flirting, he drifted off into the crowd, enveloped by some other boy's arms. I turned away, feigning disinterest, but turned back only moments later.

He was gone.

On the way out of the club, as Harlan and I helmeted up beside my bike, he shook his head.

"I'm telling you, that boy is truu-bull."

"I know, I know," I agreed. "I just wanna put him in my zine. He's perfect."

"Perfectly rabid."

"You did him?"

"What do you think?"

"Doesn't seem your type."

"Which is?"

"You know, your usual, huge, buffed and vanilla, no sprinkles."

"We all have our little diversions," he said, as I watched Harlan's ass straddle the seat of my bike. I felt him against my back for the remainder of our ride to our separate homes.

Diversion, I thought. More like a ten-car pile-up, that one. I guess that's why they make us wear helmets.

Initially, Griffin and I were to meet at what I prefer to call the Caffeine Black Hole.

Where else can you make a date with someone, only to encounter someone else you'd rather not see, say an ex-boyfriend or disgruntled former roommate. You may not sit with them, but through the tight and cramped collision of seats and tales, any shred of conversation is imparted to any number of faux-artistes, scribbling away in their unlined "journals" or pretentiously clicking away on their Powerbooks while sipping the tepid dregs of their double lattes.

I do not write in public. That I consider a holy and private act, one which demands that I live alone, now that this opera has played itself out, a condition in which I have spent a majority of my time, a self-imposed exile, a recovery.

After the anticipated chit chat with useless members of the faux-arts scene, I was able to pull Griffin away from the den of caffienedom.

We went to Duboce Park, a brief expanse of sloping lawn only a few blocks up Noe Street. Since the sun was out and, since so many people let their dogs run there, it seemed appropriate.

Clouds raced by above as dogs scampered up and down the sloping hill, catching balls, shitting, sniffing about.

Before I even had my camera out, he was ready.

"Hey, check these out," Griffin said, pulling his jeans down low to reveal the edge of a pair of boxer shorts, white with little black dog silhouettes. I was charmed and thrilled. He knew me too well.

"Let's get some color shots."

I was like some awkward photographer in those stilted Bob Mizer physique films, the geek ogling over his studly model, unable to stare at the young body without a camera between them.

As the designer and cocreator of a few small gay magazines, I'd had years of graphic arts experience under my belt, but every time I had to shoot some cute guy, I felt like the high school yearbook photographer I once was, awkwardly sneaking shots of the school jocks on the playing field.

It was when I zoomed in close to get a shot of his undershorts, those silly boxers with dogs on them, that I stared at his flat nearly hairless belly. A few hairs twirled around his dent of a navel, trailing down underneath the boxer shorts. My dick stiffened in my pants.

The wind blew a gust and I felt embarrassed, feeling so sexual out in the open with lesbian moms strolling by, their babies in carriages.

A dog came by and sniffed us a moment, then was off in search of his ball.

I took more pictures, all the while amazed at Griffin's comfort in front of a camera. He knew he was cute, in a strange way, compelling, and he dealt with it, doled it out in doses, just enough to make me want more.

And while many of the pictures, now stored away to keep me from pining over them for long afternoons, captured his handsome frame, and his slightly developed chest, it was one shot, a casual instant caught midair, that I used for the cover of my zine. In a moment, I tossed a Frisbee to Griffin, and as if he had been trained all his young life to accomplish it, with a sudden carelessness, he caught the disc between his teeth, midair.

I knew we would end up making love. I knew I would fall in love. I wanted to hold off, not unlike the days in college when, with a sex-filled date looming in the weekend, I refrained from even masturbating, my stiffening boners exhausting me with their need. I wanted to hold off as long as possible.

I refused to go after Griffin, and refused to dive in. I knew, somewhere inside, how quickly my friendship would turn into obsession, and for that I was scared.

Nevertheless, I fell prey to vanity, and asked for the ever-buffed Harlan's assistance in the gravest of sacrifices. I joined his gym.

Harlan relented to take me through his routine, a place I loved and hated. It was great to feel the effects of the workouts, and to see all the guys naked in the showers and changing room, but there was something creepy about it all, the way guys watched you, judging you by muscle groups, barely making chit chat, all working for some impossible fascist ideal of a perfect body.

There were joys to be had, of course; the silent longing flirting glances, the glorious looks as men showered, the water cascading off their bodies, streaming down the tips of their cocks, cut, uncut, a few even Prince Albert-ed. Bent over asses, arms scrubbed with towels, everyone on display, so nonchalant, so uptight.

I enjoyed showing off my lean frame, the muscles taut from years of doing very little except eating anything and sweating from riding or running, cycling or sex. I like showing myself off. I like getting my cock as erect as is decently possible, maybe ducking into the steam room, where a stiff erection merely gets a glance, where no one cares, where everyone licks his lips.

There was the tall lanky doctor/basketball player who loved to weigh himself after emerging erect from the steam room. There was the tightly muscled short furry Spanish gymnast who did pull-ups with his legs pointing out. His mustache promised sexual revolution. I especially loved watching him shower. He liked to bend over and scrub his feet a lot. Before toweling off, he also wiped the sheets of water from his compact frame. I also grew up doing that, and every time it made me think of him, and those scrapers the Greeks used on oiled-up wrestlers.

But he was a man in control, not a pup at all. Others like him weren't the real reason for my return to the torture chamber. I wanted to be in shape. I wanted to get toned, get some muscles, something to grab onto.

I lied to myself, saying it wasn't for Griffin. But even though we hadn't so much as kissed, I knew I wanted to be good for him. It was like I was preparing for a strenuous, death-defying mountain climb, and I needed Harlan's help.

Since he'd been working out for about five years, Harlan's body naturally drew stares wherever he went. It didn't hurt that he wore tight bicycle shorts and a skimpy sleeveless t-shirt. He wasn't huge, but sculpted, toned and beautiful. I'd long ago given up trying to get him into bed. Harlan likes his friends and his sex partners separate. I don't understand it, but it's just one of his eccentricities that I tolerate for the gift of his special, undying friendship, something that always outlasts any affair.

"So, tell me more about Griffin," I said between biceps curls.

"I told you. Trouble. T-R-U-B-L."

"Why?"

"He likes to fuck around, and I know you are husband-hunting."

"Not necessarily."

"Darling, it's in your blood. What is that line you always quote from *Tales of the City?* I fell in love…"

"…four times on the bus today. Yeah, yeah, yeah. Well, I don't take the bus anymore."

"Yeah, and maybe I wanna become a chubby chaser."

"How is he in bed?" I asked bluntly.

"Phenomenal. A total slut. We did everything."

"Meaning?"

"What do you think it means? I mean, everything that I do. He had some pretty raunchy suggestions, but I only have so many bedsheets."

"Ew, you mean...?"

"No, not that, but just about everything else. I'm telling you, he's not for you."

"Thanks for the warning, Blanche."

Like the barbell, I let it drop, but I knew Harlan wasn't going to stop me. He'd seen me crash on would-be boyfriends before, and by now he'd become a sort of sports commentator to my every wrong turn, like that Scottish guy on the ABC wide world of drag racing. Just another spin out. Get the fire extinguishers.

3

"Rape me."

It was our first date. Well, I don't think he thought it was a date, since we went with two other guys. Nirvana was doing a benefit for the rape victims of Bosnia. L7, Disposable Heroes of Hiphopracy and the Breeders were also playing at the Cow Palace, a huge arena usually reserved for rodeos and monster truck rallies. It was going to be mosh pit mania, and I knew Griffin was the perfect guy to go with.

Harlan had invited our friend Lee, who conveniently had a car, and I wouldn't be up to riding on my motorcycle, considering the amount of pot I wanted to smoke. I value my buzzes, but I value Rose, my Honda, more. Besides, Harlan had bought the four tickets together, and it was his idea. It seemed a nice way to start things off, be with Griffin among friends, to sort of test him out. Double dating, safe as chewing gum.

By the time Nirvana came on, Griffin and I had gotten high, drunk a beer, wandered the terrain of the Cow Palace, pissed next to each other in a toilet stall, peeked at each other's dicks, cruised other guys and even a few girls, but mostly we moshed.

Kurt Cobain started off with "Rape Me," and it was blunt and shocking. I think most of the kids in the bin of dancing cheering bodies got it, the irony of his lyrics. The others were dangerous head cases. We managed to stay away from them.

We whirled around in the sweaty mob, being shoved back and forth, grinning stupidly amid the happy crowd.

Rarely losing sight of each other, when we did, some kind of honing instinct brought us back together. We mapped our territory with a few distinct tall heads. It was a bumpy blanket of sweaty flannel, and we bounced and rocked for a while, but then after a while, we merely stood close, bumping up and down, singing along.

Griffin was in front of me when I bumped up closer to him, and he reached around behind and grabbed my crotch, then reached further and shoved my groin up against him. I could smell him, his scent mixed in with the heat of a few thousand others. I got hard. In the midst of the crowd, I was mashing my hard dick, inside my jeans, up against his butt. We held hands under the safety of the dark arena. Besides, I thought, if anyone had a problem, we could just get in a big fight right there.

But that wasn't the energy of the crowd. I never had a problem in mosh pits. The whole arena was awash in homo superiority. Weren't we all watching the rock world's latest honorary homosexual rasp out song after song?

For almost the entire concert, except for a few more swirls in the mosh pit, he stood in front of me, close, my boner bumping his rear, me stealing licks of his neck sweat.

We met up with Harlan and Lee in the parking lot, where we'd stolen a kiss. We spent the whole ride back feeling each other up, giggling, and only occasionally being polite enough to engage in the conversation of our friends, who raved about Hiphopracy's flying sparks, Cobain's flying leap into Dave Grohl's drum set.

Once, I caught Harlan looking back from the front seat with a glint of maternal approval. I had my hand up the leg of Griffin's jams, his baggies an open invitation to glide up his smooth thigh and shake hands, for the first time, with his cock. I thought it appropriate that this first moment had an audience.

Finally, we got to Griffin's house in Bernal Heights.

"Let's get together," he whispered into my ear before licking it.

"Okay," I giggled.

"Tomorrow."

"Great."

"I'd invite you over, but..."

"No, no, tomorrow's fine. I'll see you."

"Okay."

I watched him unlock his door and glance back with a grin as we pulled away.

"Well, that certainly got off to nice start," Harlan remarked. I sat in the back seat, grinning like a kid.

"Are you going out again?" Lee asked.

"Duh!"

4

Our first real date was the next day. Easter Sunday.

We didn't go to mass.

I should say that I am not Catholic. The holiday means nothing to me, more than pajama chocolate binges and big breakfasts cooked by my mother. My childhood tribute to Jesus' death and resurrection was a slow reading of the Sunday papers, followed by the ritual fireplace melting of Easter grass.

Yet the Catholic taste has woven its way into my life. Certainly the guilt part, as you'll discover, but also my sense of design. Take the fireplace in my rented apartment. Not functional, of course. How could it be with my CD cassette TV complex (loaned by Harlan) nestled in its square mouth, the wooden ornate ledge and poles, and the above shelf, festooned, no, cluttered with mementos of my first visits to beaches and bars. They don't see this, the ones who involuntarily make a donation when I borrow a trinket from their bureaus, or save a movie stub, a pebble or a dried flower bud, a lost earring; mementos of San Francisco would litter my New York apartment after I'd returned.

I mention this, because the first time I entered Griffin, slid my cock up behind him, he was standing before my shrine, my fireplace.

Dinner was a blur. Baghdad Cafe. We were under glass, in a fishbowl, a score of homos passing by to admire the fire between us. I think the food was good. The thing that excited me was how we couldn't stop talking, about anything. So much in common, not in common, laughing at each other's opinions with a recklessness that glared. It didn't matter. We were going to fuck that night, in my home, I knew it, and for that, I overtipped the surprised waitress.

He rode behind me on Rose, clutching, for the first time, but it felt as if my jacket had already worn grooves just the size of his arms. Once home, we were naked soon enough.

The shock of seeing him walk to me after going to the bathroom, that is what I remember, how so little real muscle could be so perfectly formed on his frame. Nothing was outstanding, but as a whole, he was a small god, a faun with pure sensual intent. His eyes burned. His cock danced with his balls as he strode to me.

"Hi."

"Hi."

We kissed, tender at first, for about a minute, then jaws wide open, digging down, hands pawing back muscles, down to hips and butt cheeks, grabbing, falling off center, yet both still standing, dancing as our cocks bumped hip bones.

Each of us seemed to savor it. This is the first time I will feel his belly. This is the first time I will bite his shoulder. This is the first time I will kneel before his erection. This is the first time.

We'd stood to get condoms after finally conceding to fall to kneeling, then rolling around on my bed, lying in each other's arms, licking and sucking like crazy, our new tastes sending each of us closer to shooting. I could fit his whole cock in my mouth, and the back of his throat resisted at first when I plummeted my dick down into him.

His hands pawed my ass, and a wet finger found its way into my asshole. I grabbed his solid thighs, pulled them around to smother the sides of my head, and trailed my tongue along the crevice of his scrotum, down, or up, since his ass seemed to rise up to meet my tongue, where it burrowed inside, welcoming his fresh-washed hole, tasting him end to end.

I want to ejaculate all over him, see my come clarify like butter on the heat of his chest.

But we wanted to fuck, and Griffin got up to meet me as I got the condoms out of a little box on the shelf, as if we couldn't stand to be apart for a moment.

Next thing I knew, I was caressing his ass as he placed his hands wide on the mantle, as if awaiting arrest and search. He looked at me through the inset mirror above the mantle, and I rubbered up, lubed up, stepped behind him and shoved it in.

"Ow, man. Shit."

"I hope not," I joked, and continued shoving my stiffy up him.

With some guys, I often sense resistance, fear about fucking. It makes sense. I get that feeling too, and the result is usually a softened cock.

With Griffin, it was stiff time, all the way. Trust, Risk, and Desire. We eventually crumpled to the floor, him on all fours, me clutching his cock underneath.

But I wanted *him,* not just any butt to slam my cock into, and I rolled him over, one leg over my shoulder, and pumped harder, now that we could both see it, our fucking, we hardened further, and I crouched down to kiss him.

He took my one hand that I wasn't using for support and brought it to his cock, just at the moment his moans and grunts forced their way into my mouth. His sperm splattered over my hand. His torso quivered, his moans singing down my throat. Dripping with his come, I grabbed his cock and jerked it beyond his orgasm, until he spasmed uncontrollably and my cock flopped out of his ass. "Ohh, messy," he said as a bit of our combined lube, ass fluids and a bit of shitty juice oozed out. He jumped up with the velocity of a deer and ran into the shower, me chasing him behind. He warmed up the water while I peeled the rubber off and dropped it into the trash. I joined him under the hot spray of my old-fashioned claw-toed tub. We clung close, lathering each other up, and he knelt before me, soaping my cock, then digging a digit into my ass. He was determined to make me come on him, and I was determined to let him.

As the moment of my ejaculation approached, I saw him reach over to the faucet, and just as I shot, he hit the faucet, forcing a hotter, burning spray of water to wash over me.

My eyes burned from trying to keep them open under the water, to see his manipulations of my cock, to see where the globs of sperm clung to him, while all the others fell away, invisible on the white tub, or drizzling on the clear shower curtain, running down the sides, caught with the other water, where it swirled into the drain.

"Wow," one of us said.

He rose, and we kissed, and finished bathing, and dried each other off in the steam of the bathroom, then darted, feigning a freezing chill, and ducked under the covers.

We half slept, half grazed our fingers over each other's chests and faces, noticing small parts, between fingers, soft creases at the bend of his arm, the odd sprouts of hair on my arms, and the soft down of my belly.

He smelled slightly of a cologne, but not as if he'd put it on for me, more like he did it at the beginning of the day, and by the time we came together the second time, lying in bed, it mixed in warmly with his underarm smells and heat.

I liked it, and sniffed it and licked as we humped torsos, our cocks mashed down between our hips.

We resolved to gripping each other's cocks, daring the other to come first. It was as if our first fuck were so exciting we each had to jack each other off just thinking about it.

I kept my eyes open that time, just staring at his face, wondering what color his eyes were.

Satiated, we lay back, grazing fingers down bellies, over shoulders.

"How 'bout some of that chocolate?" he asked. I leaned over and retrieved a Cadbury egg. We nibbled on a rabbit ear.

"Happy Easter."

"Yeah, right. Downright pagan," I giggled as he licked my nipple. His tongue left a smudge of chocolate that he regarded like a small painting, then licked away.

"Did you ever go Sunday mass on Easter?" he asked.

"No."

"Well, that's something we have in common." His grin became a gate to another mystery.

"Are you not into the god thing?" I asked.

"Oh, sure. Just not that one."

"You know, with your looks, and that grin, you should be in that LeStat movie they're making."

His grin widened to what almost became a comment, but he held it, a secret, and nestled his mouth into my neck, jokingly sucking and biting. I writhed in surprise, enjoying the wet slurps and pricking teases of his teeth.

Of course, he didn't have fangs. I merely dreamt that one night. His teeth were two simple rows of smooth ordinary human teeth, perhaps filed down for pedestrian life. No, I am being cruel, fantastic, but that is what became of my imagination over the next few months, on those many days where he would disappear, only to swoop down on me in the street, and spend days with me, or call on a morning and convince me to take the day off, doing nothing with him, naked, in my home or his, or under trees, or the sky, or the moon.

5

I was pleased, but a bit surprised when he wanted to set a date again, only three days away.

He brought a bottle of wine, more expensive than I thought he could afford with his assistant chef's pay. He didn't seem to mind that I stripped him naked before even opening the bottle.

I decided to take my time. Having plunged my cock insistently inside him the first time, I was determined to tease myself.

His butt was almost incongruous to the rest of his body, which was lean, tanned and smooth, with a slight trace of hair on his legs, sternum and pits. His pubic patch he regularly trimmed, but it didn't seem coy or plastic like others. It fit him.

But that butt, those glorious cushions, pale inside the strict borders of his tan line, often glowed in the night. They were the color of cream with a hint of coffee, and unblemished. Flexed, they resembled a white valentine. Relaxed, his butt was rarely noticeable under his baggy pants, but naked, they flexed and relaxed as I followed him into the shower, into the bed.

The way I fucked Griffin, the long times, wherein I'd already made him come, or pressed his arms up over his head to keep him off his dick or slurp his arm pits, I'd get too close to ejaculating up inside him. To hold off, I merely had to pull away from Griffin, stop licking his back, stop running my fingers through his hair, and just pump my dick in and out, watch it, appraise the angle, like a director, or maybe think about where I'd rather be while fucking Griffin, on a grassy highway median in Pennsylvania, atop Mount Sutro, or even in a basement. It wouldn't just be in my or his bed.

And then I'd quiver, my cock starting to pulse on its own, not a tingle like the jets of come eager for a blastoff, but the oozy, creamy globs that just take their time to crawl out of your piss slit. I wondered whether I would prefer to do this inside him, or along some body part, his ass cheek, his thigh, his neck. Where would I like it best, where was the most prime platter on which to lick my sperm?

We got out of bed, starving, remembering the wine. I cooked naked, and he poured the wine naked, and we ate naked. There was no one to tell us no, no one to tell us that now we must be decent, now we must be merely talking, not craving like beasts.

Dinner was settling on our plates; chicken, fleshy, warm, with potatoes making lava pools of gravy. We nibbled and half finished, and then I took the bottle and the two glasses and led him into the living room.

Sipping my glass, I held a gulp of wine in my mouth, then knelt and took his cock in my mouth. The sensation made him cringe. It was warm and red, but burned his skin. Yet I held his hips at the pale untanned area, the soft bones protruding like handles, and felt him grow hard as I swallowed, bit by bit, the warm bittersweet wine.

His cock was not huge, but a charming weapon of thrusts and teasing tastes, and although we often switched positions when fucking, it was his rear that seemed to lead to all other nerves, all sensations.

It was his butt that would eventually lead me to obsession, and the shock of his infection.

In the awkward morning, we made no specific plans for another date, but when I asked when I'd see him again, he said, "Keep one eye lookin' over your shoulder."

"An integral part of any relationship
is knowing that you could be
killed in your sleep at any time."

– Trent Reznor

6

Harlan invited me over a few days after that. He was having a little get-together, one of his "dinner and bootleg video" nights, where his friends from Britain sent him some of the good comedy shows with queer bits and such. Usually we downed a good wine, ate a good meal, and ended up on his bed watching the tube, stripped down to our shirts and shorts. San Francisco's weather demanded it, when it wasn't coated in a slew of rain clouds or fog.

Our loose family included Denton and Vic, the loving couple in Harlan's close circle of friends. Denton was our age, typical "just hit thirty mood swing uber-butch yet still able to whip up a gourmet dinner at a moment's notice" homo. His most visible obsession, besides pumping his body to large proportions, was his ritual weekly flat-top touch-up that made people stare as if a sex-crazed Marine had accidentally wandered into the Castro.

Vic was Denton's daddy, his boyfriend, his mate. Vic had silver hair in a brush cut that made any man want to run his fingers, and other things, through it. They were not sexually monogamous, but definitely emotionally monogamous. They had an apartment I'd found for them on Diamond Street, near the Castro. I couldn't take the apartment when I saw it. It was just too happy.

It felt comfortable to be in Harlan's bed. I always got there early so I could steal a few sniffs of his sheets, do the dish, and generally soak up as much of his hunkitude as I could before things got too campy. Harlan and I took the bed, and Denton and Vic were entangled on Harlan's rumpled couch. We were going to watch *Poison*.

We'd finished dinner, and before the movie, during commercials in between *X-Files,* the talk got around to Griffin.

"So, are you seeing him again?" Denton asked.

"I hope so." I'd prayed to all the pagan gods that would listen.

We'd long ago gotten relaxed enough to divulge each other's sexual exploits down to the last detail. It was brotherly in a way, lying on Harlan's bed and talking about sex. At one point Denton and I ended up pilfering his selection of porno mags that he'd had donated by a friend who was moving. The atmosphere was flickering with sexual energy, as if we could devolve into a four-way orgy. But it wouldn't happen. We were family.

Naturally, it caused me endless amounts of frustration.

I settled for rubbing Harlan's back.

"Scratch it. I'm itchy."

"Been to the bacon strip too much," I chided him.

"The what?" Vic asked. He was a bit older, sort of out of synch with our trendy names and catty comments. I admired that.

"You know, Dolores Park," I explained.

"The queer tier," Denton said.

"Oh," Vic got it. "Speedo Ridge."

I scratched Harlan's back, feeling the claylike warmth of him, saving the sensation for later in my lusty loneliness.

"Oh, I wanna go."

"If the sun ever comes back out."

"Hey, it's April," Denton reminded us.

I smiled, recalling the day when my sister called from Connecticut. "What are you doing?" I'd asked.

"Shoveling the Volvo out of the snowdrift that is my driveway," she'd grumbled.

I didn't tell her I'd swam in the Pacific on a beach with a dozen naked men. She'd always say, "Stop bragging," and I'd make her feel bad about not staying back in Cali after college.

Distracted, I massaged a bit too hard.

"Owee," Harlan whined in a faux-Brit boy manner that I found excruciatingly endearing.

"You'll get his little skin cells under your fingernails," Denton said.

"You could take me home and make a clone of me," Harlan joked.

"Make one of you that says yes," I blurted.

Everyone laughed, because it was too true. They all knew how much I wanted Harlan, at least between my periods of boyfriend attempts, like Griffin. I didn't want them to make it crash down with their opinions, yet I wanted their approval, wanted to be able to bring Griffin into the ranks of close lovers and friends. I wanted to extend the family. That's how it was with us.

And yet I knew it wouldn't ever really happen. As much as they frustrated me, and occasionally hurt me with their constant withholding of sex, they did it for a reason, to provide the only shred of family I had in this fog-shrouded land of broken affairs and manicured sundecks. And they saw, more than I, the eventual crash of my desires.

"So, how's Griffin?" Denton asked, eager for juicy details.

"Okay."

"Just okay."

"Yeah. We date, you know. He's nice."

"Come on, tell us everything."

"Confess! Confess! Confess!" Harlan and Denton were on top of me, grabbing me, laughing, while Vic watched in bemusement. Boys. It was as if they couldn't stand my keeping a secret, but I couldn't tell them, couldn't air the beauty of Griffin, his sting, his spell. It couldn't be shared.

I finally satisfied them with, "The sex is really good and we like each other and that's all there is to it."

"So, why don't you invite him over sometime?" Vic asked.

I glanced at Harlan. He knew. A dinner party? Sure, like, let my new dear friends peck and poke and then turn in a judgment, saying, We think he's not good enough for you. Or even worse: We want to fuck him too. Share your toys.

"Yeah, bring him over for dinner," Denton said. I could see the drool forming at the back of his mouth.

"I don't think so."

"Why not?"

I wanted to end the discussion, push off their hunger. "He's not really housebroken yet."

7

If you've ever seen the episode of *Absolutely Fabulous* where Patsy and Edina actually go to an editorial meeting, then you know what it's like for me to sit through a staff session with my editors at the gay magazine where I worked. Take away the British accents, replace the cast with a few snippy sweater queens, a loping leather daddy and a perky sports dyke, and you've got the staff I worked with. Four editors, fourteen opinions on everything. Lots of "lovely photos."

Of course I wasn't paying attention to their banter. I just nodded, sure. I'd design their Shocking Bland vision of Gay World to increase readership, design the issue to death, which would cheerfully adorn the coffee tables of homos around the country, bang out another lovely design for the cultural elite. No problem.

I'd already stolen enough supplies and Photostat time to arrange the boards for DOGZ, the West Coast issue that, it seemed, was going to be devoted to Griffin. All I was really worried about was getting back to that certain caller, whose only message was, "Woof."

"Hey," I said, as soon as my compatriots released me from the meeting.

"Tonight?" he said.

"Sure."

"Whaddaya wanna do?"

I was flustered. I wanted to impress him, keep him entertained. Too pretentious, and I'd blow it, or not get to blow him. I grabbed a copy of a local rag, and saw an ad for a movie at the Castro Theatre that was gay-esque but wasn't too horrible.

He accepted.

Rose was having a fit with her starter, so I had to run to the theater to get tickets. I forget the film. Another "touching drama" that made queers wind around the block to see it, since they only showed it for one day, while the rest of the year was gargantuan classics retread, "with new Dynachrome sound! Director's Cut!"

I do remember the tingle of waiting in line, not worried about the lost extra six bucks if he didn't show, just nervous that at any moment he'd start the pulling back, the "Oh, I'm sorry, I can't make it" shit.

But he swooped down on me just as I was about to give up.

I held his hand in the theater, hung my arm over his shoulder until it fell asleep, pressed my leg along his, anything just to keep touching him. Anything to keep the others, the predators, at bay.

We walked home. It was nice to hold hands along Noe, that brief safe area where gay-bashers rarely tread. Even so, it gave me the tickle of my life being with him, being his for the night, seeing the nods of assent from other men, saying silently, "You two are together, and we like to see that."

At one point he just grabbed me and pulled me to him along the wall of some building. We kissed right there, as if he were tempting repercussions.

We got to Duboce Park. The sky opened up for us, the glow of the Safeway sign illuminating the night.

We sat on the grass for a bit, but then the sprinklers started, and for a moment I thought he might want to run through them, but at least a sliver of logic came to him as he led me off the grounds. Somebody's Labrador ambled by.

We sat on one of the benches where an occasional homeless person parked. No such folk that night. A huge pine tree hung behind the bench, its branches occasionally tickling our backs.

We sat, kissed, and he didn't wait more than a minute before he fished down into my pants and started toying with my cock.

His hand was cold and wet from the grass, but it warmed up as my cock's skin tugged back with his yanks. I reached my hand up inside his shirt to feel his strong little back. We smooched. Couples of all genders strode by, bemused.

But then he knelt down and unzipped my pants, sucking me right out there in the open. I tried to refrain from any Puritan impulses, and only pulled his head up moments before a couple came by in the darkness. I yanked my sweat shirt over my crotch, my cock still stiff, outside my pants.

We waited for the couple to pass, then I too grabbed for his penis, which was stiff, and slurped away at it, hoping he'd at least find the same reserve I did.

But as I became drunk with the sound of his cock slurping in and out of my mouth, I heard footsteps approach. Another couple, only a few feet from us, both glanced in shock at the sight of Griffin's cock, pale in the night light, jutting up from the folds of his pants. I looked away until the couple passed.

"You're insane," I whispered as I grabbed his dick. We yanked each other's dicks, and it wasn't a few more moments before we both ejaculated all over our pants.

We giggled and moaned at the absurdity of it, the hissing of the sprinklers hiding our sounds. My cock still pointed out from inside my pants as we strode homeward, our sperm dribbling down our pants.

When we got home, the evidence of our obvious come stains only inspired us to have sex again.

"This time, I fuck you," he said as we shucked off our stained clothes.

"No problem." I clicked on a CD, Chris Isaak. Perfect fucking music.

I went into the bathroom, cleaned out my ass as best I could, then found Griffin standing naked except for white socks, rolling a rubber over his dick. No prelims. I just got on all fours. He slapped my butt a few times, then got down, shoving his nose between my butt cheeks. I heard the soft slick sounds of him lubing up his boner, then felt the gooey stiffness parking at my butt lips.

I let him go at it, knowing he liked it, and I liked the feel of him reaching around to grab my boner, which banged up against my belly, but I had to pull away. I had to see him while he fucked me.

I shoved him down on his back, right on the floor, and crouched over him, straddling him, then let his erection slide its way up inside me. I rode up and down, and he folded his arms up behind his head for a while, enjoying the view. He reached up and grabbed my dick, then started to arch his head up to try and suck me at the same time. I leaned forward. His cock flopped out of my ass.

I leaned back, re-parking on his dick. I grabbed his knees, shoving his legs back toward his head as I leaned forward again, forcing his flexible torso closer, until he had just half his cock jabbing up inside me, and his mouth made contact. We were each getting it from both ends, and as he shot up my ass. I waited, selfish, wanting to feel it all before coming on his neck, then leaning down, shoving his cock out, then collapsing to nestle in the crook of his neck and shoulder, licking, slurping, smelling my own goo, feeling our ribcages thump with blood and life.

"Oh, man, my back is gonna fuckin' hurt tomorrow."

I offered to massage it, only if he stayed the night. He accepted.

I think he made his mistake the next morning. We both woke up with piss hardons, but were too lazy to get up, and not kinky enough to just piss in each other's mouths, not that we didn't joke about it.

Instead, I ended up slurping on him, and he on my dick, and then I pawed his ass a bit and before I knew it I had a rubber on and his ass all lubed up and I was plowing away at him like a thoughtless husband, just banging away past his morning shit, shoving him down under the day's first slats of sun, then reaching under him and pulling his cock.

He grunted, clenched his muscles, then tried to adjust himself and his head on the window ledge. I rubbed his forehead, still holding my cock inside him, and yanked him back further onto the bed. He raised his ass and shoved back, and then he ended up sideways, then on top, riding me, crouching his legs at my hips, shoving his spread ass up and down and clenching, hard, the way I like it, the way he could make me come, and I knew he was ready too, and it was bliss when I shot up into him and got his jizz all over my chest and face, but he didn't collapse like I wanted.

He just sat on me, my cock still in him, and regarded my prone form, crisscrossed in sperm like an action painting. He looked at me like a kid who wants Daddy to wake up and play some more.

"Hungry?" I asked.

"Yeah."

"How 'bout some omelets and toast and fresh carrot juice?"

"Carrot juice! I love you!" He ripped his ass off my cock, slurped a wet kiss on my neck where his come lay dribbling, then raced off to the shower.

He said it. I didn't.

Sure, it was tossed off as easy as my spunk-filled rubber, but he said it.

8

Since I live alone, it was only natural that Griffin come over to my house for our nights together. My home in the Haight Valley (Somewhere between the Lower Haight and Hayes Valley. I know, it's too much) was on his way to work at a restaurant in the Polk Street district, so it worked out fine. But he always had to take the bus, and after a few nudging words about wanting to make him feel comfortable, that I wanted to come to him, he relented, having a night when his two roommates were out of town, a straight married couple who lived under him in a split-level house in Bernal Heights.

"No wild stuff at my house. I got roommates."

I consented to his request, for the time being.

Approaching his house, I chuckled to myself about the cliché notions of Bernal Heights, that it was overrun by lesbian-owned cats and free-range alfalfa groceries.

But my impression that night, and forever after, was far removed from the potluck Berkinstock stereotype. The hill of Bernal Heights, with its odd radio tower and gaunt trees jutting up from the otherwise bare mount, seemed to loom that night under the sky.

I imagined Griffin perching up there like the living gargoyle I once imagined him to be, considering taking wing, to swoop down on some unsuspecting man or small creature.

A man's home, specifically his bedroom, and his books, reveal all. People can cover up things with words and actions, but the way a person arranges their possessions, and the things they collect, can show much more than taste. For that, I love to visit men's homes, and on the times when that happens, I am silent, until after the tour, after taking it all in, like the scent of a great meal.

Griffin had heard my bike rumble up to his house, and greeted me at the door. We kissed under the porch lamp. I hoped neighbors watched. It was one of San Francisco's great little pleasures, kissing at the door without fear, usually.

The house was a slim, oddly-shaped one with no discernible age. Add-ons and bare wall met with cluttered areas. The fireplace lay dormant, the living room nearly devoid of decoration, just a simple couch, TV and a few chairs. The bookshelves were empty. That worried me.

The kitchen (he was cooking dinner) was warm and neatly arranged, with a deck that led out to a view over the small yard, lit with small mushroom-shaped lights. I immediately imagined us fucking by the jade and bougainvillea.

But the view - San Francisco spread out like a glistening purple blanket, the fog racing across the night - was magnificent.

"Beautiful," I burst out as he brought me a glass of wine. I sipped, letting it burn warmly into my mouth, then, as he lowered his glass, I kissed him.

We chatted and hugged to keep off the chill, but had to return inside. A cat strode in, dark and mottled, a medium, perhaps. I had noticed a few witchery symbols, but considered it mere goth rock affectation. Still, it was black, so I approached it with caution, until the moist triangle of its nose sniffed, then touched my hand, then rubbed affectionately. I was welcomed.

"Come see my room," Griffin said, and I remembered boyhood after-school dates, the thrill of sharing toys and trading Matchbox cars.

It was then that I fell further in love with him. The intimacy of his neat stacks of clothes in the open closet, the small library of CDs, cassettes and books were endearing.

Even more were the numerous mementos arranged on his desk and tabletops; bones, feathers, bits of rock and quartz arranged like small shrines.

There was a photo of him from Halloween, his hair spiked and dyed bright red. He wore only pants and boots with a large cape. Shirtless, he grinned with his evil joy to match the horns he had attached to his temples. It seemed the most fitting outfit, not a costume at all. People often became their true selves on Halloween.

Stretched over the wall above his bed was a wide, paint-splattered canvas, in a style that was a sort of Japanese brush paint, with darker cartoons, a torso, no two, commingling beneath the black strokes. It was sloppy and masterful, the work of an unaffected artist.

"You did this," I said.

"Yup."

"I like it. Does it have a title?"

"Not yet."

I perused his shelves: CDs, tapes, pictures, some that I had given him from the photo shoot at Duboce Park. The stickers, bones, candles, all arranged in a way I would never have allowed, my tastes demanding symmetry, but it was his. It had a scent, a casual order.

I was going to fuck and be fucked by Griffin in this room, and I savored my anticipation like the wine. Sex would be so different here, in his space. It was undefined, like we were newly met.

He put on a tape that started with one of those grunge bands popular on the local "alternative" radio station.

"I want you to notice, when I'm not around. You're so special, so fucking special, but I'm a creep, I'm a loser..."

I didn't know then how appropriate that song would be, how I wouldn't hear it without thinking of him, another stupid ditty, another piece of pop to use as a latch to the lost past.

The dinner was good, but the wine was better. I asked him if he wanted to get high. His eyes sparkled. "Outside," he muttered. "Don't wanna stink up the apartment or my roommates'll want some."

We stepped out onto the porch again to admire the view, sucking in cannabis. I felt the smoke whirl around my lungs. The high sizzled down to my groin, loosening my guts. My cock began to feel like a vine, enlarging, growing, snaking down the length of my pants.

We ended up back in his room, stripping down to just socks, since his floor was a little cold. We started in the bed, me kneeling before him as he sat on the side.

But then he led me back out to the deck, me following his pale rounded butt as we padded naked through the darkened house, and eventually, out onto the deck. I could hear the music in the house now, softer stuff, but with some guitar. It was a song by Pink Floyd. I laughed.

"What?" he said.

"Nothing. The view. It's great." I love you.

I thought of the thousands of people who would pass us that night on the highway below. To them, we were a mere blip, a small shape in the black blanket lit by the constellation of street and house lights. But that small blur was us, on that deck, in the dark, with the city sprawled out below in hills and valleys, singing to us, a low hiss and rumble of traffic and people, of doubts and misgivings, a symphony of pain and distraction.

Our socks became dirty from the wood below us, but I didn't care. We both smoked cigarettes to cut the desire awhile, to relax in it, to assure ourselves of our mission, tease ourselves.

But I eventually put out the smoke and knelt behind him while he surveyed his view. I nestled my nose in the warmth of his ass while licking down to the nub where his balls started. He quivered. My nose was cold, but it warmed as I nestled my face between his cheeks.

He shoved his not yet completely hard cock back under his legs. I nibbled the head. He turned, facing me, and I sucked him to rigidity, then slathered up, pawing, caressing, licking, and up to his face. He still tasted of cigarette, wine and pot, but I dug my tongue deep inside until I only tasted him.

Our escapade was only interrupted by a quick exit to his room for rubbers and goo. Before I had it on, he clamped his hands on the railing, ready for it.

I fucked him as he leaned against the rail. The ring of muscle accepted me as if I belonged there, always. I couldn't decide which was more beautiful, the view, or the taut action of his back muscles as I thrust in and out.

At some point, he brought one leg up, and I fiddled with his dangling balls while he jacked off. Gripping his chest, I wrapped around him with my other arm, I gave him a shove, right from the base of my cock. He lost his balance, nearly falling over the balcony, and grabbed convulsively for my neck.

I pulled back, and cooed into his ear, "Relax, baby, I gotcha, I gotcha. I'm never lettin' go."

I came, but didn't tell him, because I wanted more. I just pulled out the rubber and dropped it on the deck. Then he sat in a lawn chair, and I got another rubber, wrapped it around his cock, and sat.

He couldn't do the same to me, the threat, the scary moment, but he did pump up lovingly into me, knowing at least he could yank another orgasm out of me if he really tried. The chair squeaked and bent while he pumped up, and I lost my footing and had to instead squat over the whole chair. I didn't like that, feeling the cold aluminum arms, so I leaned back, taking him with me, and down to the dirty wood floor of the balcony.

The damn thing nearly broke before we were done (the chair, not the rubber), and our hands and feet were chilled, dead cold. Mid-fuck, we'd grab each other in the groin or armpit or tit to make each other jump in reaction from the cold fingers.

But our mouths and dicks and my butt was warm, and we humped and giggled and I knew he'd jacked off here in that very chair, which sat bent now, twisted, corrupted by our heedlessness.

I thought of him in that chair on previous nights, imagining having someone to do this to, or maybe me. I wanted to fuck away the traces of anyone else, or even doing it in that chair ever again. I wanted our every moment to be the last of its kind.

I awoke to clanging sounds outside his room. Griffin's back was facing me, and I licked slowly, rousing him to a slow bit of grunts and hip gyrations. He reached behind for my head and shoved it down. I skied along the curve of his spine, down to the globes, caressing them, biting, shoving my head under and between his legs until he parted them, then I emerged at his crotch, sucking the sweet salt of our night sweat. Sucking cock in the morning is great, a perfect excuse not to kiss. Since your breath reeks of forgotten dreams, it's the only way to say, "Good morning."

As we rearranged ourselves into a tight 69, our cocks just being in each other's mouths, not insistently pumping, I heard the roommates outside, talking, making breakfast. It sounded like they wanted us to hear, but we felt like boys, our parents outside not knowing, or knowing, what we were up to.

I wanted to come with Griffin's cock in my mouth, so I pulled out of his jaws, reluctantly, and started squeezing and tugging my penis, shoving the head of it against the valley below his Adam's apple. I spewed slow and oozy, and choked myself on his cock, then he quivered a moment, and I almost took it, ate it, but shoved myself aside, down to his balls and scrotum, digging a finger in his ass, obeying the rules, partially. He let me feel him splooge against my chest.

We relaxed, entwined, exhausted and energized at the same time. I held my face against his thigh, so solid and warm. He toyed with a few of my ass hairs, then plucked one out, forcing me to sit up.

"Hey, stop it."

He plucked another.

I grabbed him, we wrestled, and I forced his face into the puddle of his own spew, shoving his head down until he licked me clean.

We tugged on shorts, then padded to the bathroom, but were caught, dicks half hard, jutting forward, denting our undies, by a tall, longhaired man in black jeans, black T-shirt and bare feet. There was a tired morning look in his eyes. He had a dark goatee that would have been sexy, had he not looked so damned boringly heterosexual, like, I don't even want to know what you guys do.

"Hurry up," was all he said.

"The roommate?" I whispered under the hiss of the shower.

"None other," Griffin nodded as we hugged under the spray. We lathered each other up, me kneeling before his cock, then turning him and soaping up the glorious butt. He did the same. I felt exalted, tingly, perfect. Loved, adored. Starving.

"Does he cook?"

"No. Maybe there's coffee."

"Good."

We returned dressed, to the kitchen.

Steve and Donna Pilan, or Pillan, I forget. I think they forgot my name as soon as they heard it. They both wore black.

Donna was a bit more cheerful, kind of dreamy-eyed, a fair dusty blond drape of hair adorned her slightly freckled face. She had a small frame, but nice contours, pretty enough to stir my occasional sliver of bisexual desire.

"Nice bike ya got," Steve said.

"Thanks."

"Course it's not a Harley."

"No. It's not."

"Coffee?" Donna asked.

"Thanks."

They both worked, he an architectural draftsman, her a marketing rep for some eco-friendly mail order catalog. I bid them a good day, but as they trundled off in his pickup, I couldn't help but feel relieved.

They don't like me, I thought. They resent Griffin having me over.

I joked for a moment that they were a coven, and Griffin's face opened up, as if I had revealed some secret.

"No," he laughed it off. "But we might as well be."

I'd seen the picture of him at Halloween, looking like the most convincing lower demon. His friends did all wear black.

But it wasn't an evil thing, at least I didn't think so. It was more homey, like kids who listen to too much Jane's Addiction. It was Satanism as style, a more sophisticated version of the spray-painted scrawls of five pointed pentacles that cluttered up the walls of abandoned buildings, decorated by kids overdosed on Blue Oyster Cult. It was innocuous evil, a light-hearted romp. But like the remnants of any myth, the real pulse of it lay trickling beneath, like a lost stream under caves.

9

As much as I enjoyed the view, I pretty much took to inviting him over to my place, since in my sanctum, no one can hear you scream while you're getting impaled. Well, maybe a neighbor or two, but I think they like it.

I'd grown brave in my givings to him, my Griffin, and he was mine, for a time. There came nights where my candles sputtered, and he merely adjusted the shade to allow the night streetlight slats of silver to graze his chest as he rode my cock.

I sat on the red comfy chair, one of those sodden dilapidated wide-armed Deco things in desperate need of a reupholster. But I wouldn't dare. This was Harlan's old "by the phone" chair. You know what that means.

No, not paid phone sex. See, Harlan's positive, and something in him, he said, knows if we ever get together, it would be "swallow the splash" night, and he doesn't want to see his friends get positive like him.

I like to think that. It's better than the simple fact that Harlan only goes for big muscled, huge-titted boys with brains like gophers, I reminded myself, as if I would ever learn.

My tits are between my legs, I say. Fuck my tits.

And just that he did, my Griffin, in the chair Harlan had more often than I knew, jacked off to the voices of boys that blew off dates, wanted to just be friends, but boys he still had a nut for.

I do hate to end on prepositions. They cling to the rug like cum drops.

Which is why I would never redo that chair. In it I jumped on Griffin too, and watched as a neighbor watched, and didn't care. It was R-rated. All he saw was my up-and-down, and the back of Griffin' head, more than enough to spill juice over.

I did, on the window itself.

It was as if we deserved it, an audience, for our passion was just a bit too much for only two people. We deserved to be watched, even sleeping.

After that night, I figured we were close. Each other's. That's all I ever wanted.

At a certain point, through my suggestion, we began to expand beyond the privacy of our bedroom walls and rushed breakfasts, normal goings-out, you might call it. I wanted to go with him, to be his in public.

The night in Duboce Park had been his way of showing his real desire, to do it outdoors, in public, under the sun and God and everybody.

Unsatisfied with my giggling confessions to Harlan and Lee, I wanted the whole scene, the ragtag, sneering truckload of foghead Frisco fabulism to see us together and grin in envy.

When I went out with Griffin, he controlled his little fits and starts of impatience as he joked with one handsome guy after another. I tried to avoid categorizing these guys into three groups: Before Me, After Me and Never.

It usually got me a bit stirred up, since I never asked, so by the time we got home, I was ready to prove myself, make him forget all the Before Me's and push off as many of the After Me guys as he could for as long as possible.

It wasn't easy, putting ourselves out there for my friends' perusal and judgment. They could all see it, I realize now, the need, the compulsion, the eerie closeness we shared for a time. It was doomed to be shredded by their opinions and jealousies, and my own.

I thought I would be the one to be in charge, the one holding the leash, but there was no leash. He'd brought me down to dog level, and we just kept playing, rolling over each other, so to speak.

Bark.

I'd been staying late at work, pretending to toil away on the latest photo essay on designer homes of transgender 12-step AIDS caregivers overcoming child abuse.

I waited until everybody left so I could bang out some stats of DOGZ images, get my boards together and drop them off at my favorite copy shop, where the stringy multiple-pierced punk boy promised to give my product extra special attention (meaning no upside-down pages this time), in exchange for a few signed copies of the zine. I left the copy shop after he made a first test run. It looked good.

Eager to share my craft with my muse, I brought the copy home to give to Griffin, merely saying I had a "leetel su-prize."

"Whadja do, shave your cock?"

"I said a *little* surprise."

When he came over with a pizza, I guessed he didn't want to be outdone by my "surprise." He seemed to enjoy it. He jumped up and down. I kissed him.

"How many copies ya gonna make?"

"A hundred and one."

"Why a hundred and one?"

"Dalmatians."

"Oh. You're twisted."
"Yeah, and I don't even have a dog."
"What about me?"

At night, after fucking each other (the balance made me very happy), I often left the blinds open a bit so I could trace the constellation of freckles on Griffin's back by the slats of streetlight that bled onto my bed. I often continued grazing my fingers over his body after he'd fallen asleep. I sometimes heard a plane rumble overhead, or the distant Muni train, and for a moment, hoped it would be another grand earthquake, sent to crush us under the plaster and wood, naked, under the sheets, to die immortalized, not on the evening news, but in the verbal gossip of gay culture, the two men, entwined in each other's arms for eternity.

This is the state he put me in, no matter my attempts to remain sane through our affair. This is the flood of obsessive lust that invaded me, deadlier than the virus, the place where you lose yourself, where nothing you do matters, where every movement and action and meal alone or with others is merely in anticipation of being in his company, being whole.

10

"He's out."

Griffin's roommate, Steve the goateed het, sighed. I could hear his disgruntlement over the phone.

"How long?"

"For a few days."

"Can you take a message?"

"Why don't you just call back and leave it on the machine?"

"Sure. Fine." I hung up, but didn't do it. I didn't want this creep hearing my voice again. How could Griffin live with such an indolent character? What was going on that I didn't know?

I called a few more times, but at his roommate's whining tone, I merely hung up. After a week, I was sure he knew it was me, for before I hung up I heard him yell something about Griffin, something like "Just back off him while you can."

I wondered how close they were. Had Griffin slept with them, too?

Trying to turn Griffin into a boyfriend was like: (pick your desperate metaphor)

setting up a cozy doghouse on your back porch for a hyena.
catching the wind in an engagement ring box.
forcing a nymphomaniac into a nun's habit.
taming a rogue wolf.

Griffin was different because he had to be. He avoided the Castro scene. He usually hung out with the tattooed shave heads at a club appropriately named Fiend. It was nearly next door to the projects on Haight and Buchanan. You had to be a nasty aggressive fag to go out of that place holding hands without a scuffle. He enjoyed confrontation. I should have taken that as a warning.

We were leaving Fiend, arms over each other's shoulders. It about two in the morning. Drunk on three beers each, sweaty from dancing and humping vertically, we were distracted by our own intoxication and what we'd growled into each other's ears, something about pissing in the tub, what we wanted to do to each other when we got home.

At first we didn't even notice that the bottle that crashed in the gutter was aimed at us. Then Griffin ripped himself from me, turned and faced a herd of large men who stood, guarding, sentinels.

He stood, rigid as a hunting dog, waiting.

"You got a problem, white boy?"

"Yeah, I got a problem. Who the fuck do you think you are, throwin' bottles?!"

They came toward us as one.

"Griff, no, come on." I was ready to tear off, having survived countless catcalls from these guys, even tossed rocks when I'd rode Rose by the projects. I usually avoided the street altogether, but with him, mistakenly, I felt secure.

"We gone flatten you fagits."

Griffin dug into his pocket, pulled out a knife. I was stunned into stillness, but remembered the night I'd been bashed, back in New York, years before, while a friend, well, former friend, merely stood by and watched, horrified. I had to call my straight sister to take me to the hospital.

I extracted my house keys, quickly inserting one between each finger, ready to shred any face that got too close.

"You wanna start somethin', boy?"

"Fagit."

My heart was pumping, making me almost deaf with fear, at the same time memorizing every flicker of movement, every one of their four faces, every cadence of their voices.

"Draw blood, I dare you," Griffin growled.

"Fuckin' AIDS blood."

"Yeah, right."

"Gone pop you, fagits," one of them said, reaching for what might have been a gun. "Best be gone."

Some shred of bravery pumped out of me.

"I know all your faces," I said. "I live right down the street. One touch and guess who goes to jail. Not the white boy faggots," I said, thumping my own chest.

A cop car conveniently strolled by. The posse receded. The cop car stopped. The cops got out.

"We got a problem here?" A burly cop was between us.

"Yeah, we got a problem," Griffin said. "These goons threw a bottle at us."

"They fuckin' makin' out on our turf. Disgustin.'"

"Yeah, well, why don't you just go back to your little...houses and disappear," the cop scolded. "I'm sure you all don't wanna spend the weekend in County...again."

The cops waited with us until the posse retreated, grumbling bullshit. We decided not to press any charges. It was all a waste of time. I hated them and they hated us right back. Nothing was gonna stop that.

"You gentlemen should be more careful," the other cop said.

"Oh, like you're telling us we're not allowed to walk down the street?"

More words, cynical cop scolding. Corruption oozed from his thick face.

"Fuck this. Let's go home," I said.

Griffin took my hand, and we strolled down the street, livid, pulsing. When we got home, we simmered down, just long enough to get naked and gulp each other's piss in the bathroom, then we banged each other so hard we woke up with bruises.

11

One night at Faster Pussycat, while we were waiting for Girls in the Nose to perform, I introduced Griffin to Bobbie Bubble, the club promoter. An outlandish queen who could always be counted on to talk nonstop about his most interesting topic - himself - Bobbie was nevertheless always funny, always ready to put you on the guest list at his nightclub, Hump.

Since the San Francisco nightclub scene was, and still is, completely predictable, his ridiculous theme nights, like Wheel of Fortune (with a Vanna White look-alike contest), Temp-orama (where anyone who brought in stolen office supplies got a free drink), and the Dead Drag Queen costume contest, all were a must. I'd been slacking on covering the nightclub scene, though (I had people for that at the magazine), preferring to spend my evenings wrapped up in Griffin's arms and legs.

Bobbie recognized Griff from the swiftly selling issues of DOGZ that adorned the zine shelves of all the local stores. The lovely zine queen at A Different Light bought them up to distribute the first West Coast issue around the country. I'd made a profit of about twenty dollars, after costs.

Bobbie and Griffin hit it off so quickly I felt my stomach churn. Before their parting, they agreed to meet about some promotion deal, with Griffin as the model.

"How much?" I asked.

"Enough."

"He's a nice guy."

"He's a creep."

"But you just..."

"You have to be trusted by the people that you lie to," he said, pushing me toward the bar and through the crowd, "so that when they turn their backs on you, you'll get the chance to put the knife in."

Before the end of the month, Griffin's face was on a club invite and his nearly nude, tight little body photographed on several pages issue of *Oddity*, a trampy club rag that was free, and worth every penny.

Griffin took the small fame like a joke, but of course I didn't. My Vichy had just been invaded by Maps to the Stars Homes. Suddenly people were coming up to us to compliment him on the ad. Others talked about him at my mention of his name. Others were bragging about what they'd done with him, and the guest list was lengthy, if not amusing.

I balanced my slight jealousy with a sense of pride, but tried to avoid mentioning him to others, like a sacred secret. I didn't want to be half of anyone, at least in public.

The spring weather finally shifted from gray rain to bright sunshine, at least a few hours a day. We wanted to go out, but someplace where we wouldn't be bothered by the fickle admiration of other queens, someplace under the sun.

We rode Rose, my trusty motorcycle, to Black Sands Beach, the twisting curves of Highway 1 opening up before us, a grand spilling array of green-gray hills and shimmering ocean, flat, dotted with a few boats, and off in the distance, a freighter from China or Norway. Griffin gripped my waist as we slowed around the twisting turns, until we settled at the parking lot.

It was a warm day, and there a lot of cars, several motorcycles; Hondas, a Harley, some bicycles, too. It seemed the open sky demanded tribute.

"Have you been here before?" I asked.

"Nope," he answered as we trod down the pathway, grabbing at fennel sprouts and sage.

"You'll be happy I told you to wear your hiking boots."

It was a steep climb down, as usual, but the rocks seemed to have smoothed even more from the constant traffic of adventurous queers trekking to the most hidden away beach in the area. I got a quiver between my legs as a rock cluster crumbled under my heel.

"Whoah," Griffin hooted with a twisted glee. He enjoyed the fear. But would he trust me not to shove him down, me with him, crashing to our death? He kept a few feet away. Perhaps he read my thoughts.

We made it to the beach okay, passing Asian fishermen, who seemed not to care what the slow parade of men was doing just behind that cluster of rocks.

When we got there, a few dozen men were doing a lot of nothing. Pretending to read, lost in sunglasses and earphones, munching, smoking. A few gathered in chatty clusters, but as Griffin and I parked on a clearing at the last cove, all eyes turned to watch us take off our clothes.

It felt great to become naked in front of them, and Griffin and I shared a nasty glance as we were finally stripped, our clothes strewn about the laid-out sheet in little piles.

We straightened out our stuff, got out some water and a bit of fruit, and without a moment's hesitation, Griffin took out my pipe, dug into the little black plastic film canister, loaded a bowl, and we smoked.

The tingles shifted through my body, the ripe taste.

The scent of our pot drew heads to turn, one in particular was that of a rather well-proportioned guy with a nice tan and some light chest hair. It was nice to see some guys keeping what the goddess gave them. Between his legs, pouched in turquoise Speedos, was another natural gift. Griffin gestured to offer the stud, offering some pot, but he smiled and declined.

"Nice," he said.

"Real nice," I agreed. My jealousy rarely prevented me from enjoying our little visual flirts.

Feeling energetic and horny from the pot, Griffin and I stood and walked to the water, splashing about.

We wandered near the cave, a cozy nestled point at the farthest end of the beach, and my Black Sands luck came through again.

There was no one there, so Griffin and I wasted no time in smooching under the sun, enjoying the rush of waves at our feet, the freedom of being outside making us stiff in the breeze. Griffin knelt in the sand and swallowed my dick with his mouth.

Half-hard already, the stud who had laid nearest us came ambling along, his Speedos already dented by his hardening cock. We both spotted him, but Griffin didn't stop sucking me. I'll always remember the feeling of him turning his head, my cock in his mouth, sort of bending it, tugging it sideways, to show us off.

The guy was shy, but his cock kept getting bigger, stretching his swim suit to its limit. He edged nearer, holding back, until I gave him a conspiratorial wink and nodded for him to some closer.

He stood only inches away, watching, then leaned in and touched my shoulder, then traced his palm down my chest to the point where Griffin's mouth met my pubic bush. The stud was about to kneel as well, but I had to unveil the contents of those Speedos.

I sort of knelt, Griffin still slurping away on me, but I pulled him off so he too could witness it, that moment when, as I pulled his Speedos down, his penis, full and hard, bopped out free, bounced up and down like a springboard, and just wiggled with a life all its own.

Although we'd done just about everything two guys could do, both our cocks were nice, but only slightly above average in size. This was a massive cock, and the stud knew it. Griffin and I both marveled at its size, its girth, the contours of it. It was a cock worth choking on, a cock that made you go crazy and want to try stuffing it up your ass, despite the incredible pain, a cock to be worshipped. Griff and I lapped its sides as he jacked.

There was a tiny moment where both Griffin's and my eyes met from opposite sides of the stud's cock, marveling as it rose higher, arcing up in anticipation. Somewhere around the middle of the length of it, our lips met, and we both grunted.

Griffin and I were both sucking on him, trading drooly swipes up and down the guy's boner. We weren't even noticing him grab our heads and try to pinch our nipples. Nipples? Who cared. I was sucking a huge cock with Griffin on the other side, each of us yanking each other's puds.

The guy's knees buckled many times from our devoted licking. We traded off sucking it, shoving it in, fucking our faces with his immense dick until it hit the back of our skulls. It thrilled me to see the rounded end of his cock distorting Griffin's cheek as it banged in and out, the drool sloppily spilling out over his lips. My cock was stiffer than it had ever been with Griffin yanking it.

The poor stud couldn't help himself from falling onto the sand, the way we were both using a hand to pump him off. He tripped over his Speedos, which were still stretched taut at his calves. We knelt over him like vultures, Griffin on his balls, me on the head, impaling myself on his cock until his hand shoved my head away.

His jizz shot out in flying clots. We nudged close to fight for a splot, to get it on us, but most of it churned up in a big glob at the head of the guy's cock. When he fell back in exhaustion, Griffin kept his hand up, grabbed the guy's jizz-globbed cockhead, cupped it, coated in sperm, yanked it him a few more times as the stud's muscled furry torso convulsed in ecstasy. Then Griffin wiped the sperm all over my chest.

We laughed loud, and it echoed in the cave. We both padded on our knees, bringing our dicks to his face. But he seemed a bit scared of two cocks, and abruptly stood up.

"I gotta go," he blurted, and was off, stuffing his softening yet still huge erection into his tiny Speedos.

"Selfish bitch," Griffin yelled, and we laughed. "We should get paid for that kind of service."

"Yeah, well, I guess we might as well finish off," I said as we nestled down in the sand, clammy and cold, shoving our faces in each other's crotches, for warmth as much as the taste and feel. We shot off all over each other, then Griffin giggled and rolled himself into the sand, digging our sperm into the earth, our come lodged in like a territorial marking.

After a rest, Griff stood up to pee, but turned away. Hell, no.

I rolled over in the sand, landing kneeling before him, as he peed on my face, chest and mouth, giggling at it all.

After rinsing off in the surf, we returned to our blanket and dressed part-way, our sweatshirts tugged down over our knees. We glanced at the stud, who now lay sleeping, only once looking up to us.

We watched the water slosh and rush onto the shore, hit over the rocks, and later, as if we had deserved it, a little black bump bobbed up, then down, then sniffed. I pointed, and Griffin saw him too, the seal, the blessing. We stood, pointing and searching out into the water, all eyes on the beach admiring our postcard tranquility. When at last the seal ducked down into the surf for the last time, we strolled back, arms over shoulders, then tousled in the sand and had to rinse off again, and one of us said, "All we need now is a Labrador!"

"And a matching Jeep!"

"With a little rainbow decal."

We waited a moment, then, at the same time, shouted, "NOT!"

We were up at the parking lot, unlocking my bike, when the stud we'd had sex with "happened" to pass by on his way out. We nodded briefly, and that was it. He headed off in his car...

...a Jeep with a little rainbow flag decal on the bumper.

"No Lab?" Griffin quizzed rhetorically.

"And no matching boyfriend."

"He's at work."

"He doesn't know."

"Better yet, he knows, but he doesn't mind."

We chuckled in our feigned superiority, our remove from coupledom, from the binds and clichés, and at the same time I held my gaze on Griffin as he fitted his handsome head under my spare helmet. Yeah, I could watch him do this every night.

"You like doing it in front of others, don't you?" I asked.

He grinned in that way that said, ya got me, and I'll get you for that. "I like people seeing us together. I like sex. I like good sex with you, even with others."

"That sounds nice, almost legal," I said.

"You're not jealous?"

"Immensely," I said.

"But you liked it."

"Seeing you suck him made me hate him and love you all the more. Knowing you were watching me suck him got me even better."

"You really shot."

"Anger can be an aphrodisiac."

"Not anger, you were...fired. Like that night with the goons."

"You make me burn."

"Well, it's gettin' cold, so warm me up, Flame." He nestled close behind once I fired Rose up and dropped the kickstand. Our sweatshirts tugged down as low as possible, my gloves on, my eyes sharp. I pointed out a falcon flying high over a hill as we twisted down through the Headlands, under the dusk glow that sprawled out beyond the Golden Gate's web.

We were soon home. His home. He had to go home.

I didn't try to convince him to stay over with me. I'd had his company all day, and had to savor it.

As I was attaching his helmet to my bike, I tossed it out: "So, your roommate was really weird with me on the phone again."

"Oh him. Don't worry. They're moving out soon."

"How soon?"

"None too soon," he whispered, and looked up to his bedroom window before kissing me goodnight and heading in.

12

There is a certain moment when two men realize that they must decide. They follow the usual dating sex courtship; dinners out, movies, the theater, perhaps, or a beer bust, parties, dancing. They go home, they fuck, they wake up, they go to work, they make appointments to meet again, or they don't. That moment is never clear to some, the moment when the two conjoined paths, the intersection of which is usually the groin, when they realize it is time to move on.

The moment may pass quickly, a tired gesture while retrieving milk from the fridge, a comment made too loudly in the presence of others, a joke over the phone with the sarcasm not at all veiled, a cigarette bummed once too often. The moment is usually wordless, but understood, and soon after, the forgetting begins.

But that moment, other than my sliver of hurt that would come, did not pass in the way of my usual history of short-term affairs.

Griffin and I rarely went out like other couples, never to dinner, since he liked cooking, rarely to public occasions. When we did, something always happened to turn it into a flash point, an event, a clot of tension, a conspiracy of two, a performance.

The bar was on Polk Street, a place where he seemed too familiar. We were having Cuba Libras, me thinking it some exotic elixir, not merely a simple rum and Coke. But sitting in that bar, the older men glancing at us, Griffin whispered in my ear and it became an adventure.

"We're both hustlers on the make, looking for a three-way."

I glanced at him, consenting, and added. "Nothing less than a hundred. His place."

With that agreement, that breach into the ridiculously sordid, we separated, and wove through the crowd of older men.

Ten minutes later, Griffin nodded me over, and introduced me to a paunchy yet cheerful older man, who bought us drinks. We chatted, deepening our voices to give us a hint of violence. We flirted, laughing low and talking suggestively to give us a hint of bottom potential.

Every time Griffin and I let the older man ramble, I felt lucky that my position allowed me a direct view of the TV screen, which was showing a Pet Shop Boys video, "Young Offender."

"So, how long have you boys been in the, uh...business?"

I gave Griffin a glance, then said, "a while."

"Is this how you usually go about it?" He seemed to be fishing us out, trying to place us. We knew he wasn't a cop. Too old, but still, I was suspicious, until Griffin started talking.

"We like to work more casually. Those boys on the street. That's not our style. Gotta sleep on your toes. When you're on the street, got to be able to pick out the easy meat with your eyes closed."

He was tipsy. So was I.

Leaning in close to the guy, Griffin muttered, "Then, moving in silently, downwind, out of sight, we strike when the moment's right without thinking."

The guy finished his drink, a bit shook up, but ready, like it was now or never.

We got to his place in a cab, the older gent in the middle. We fondled his thigh. He grinned like a Cabbage Patch doll. We could have walked, since he lived in the Tenderloin, but he was paying.

The elevator took us up a lot of floors, and being slightly drunk, I was looking forward to a windy balcony with a nice view of the city, the rolling bumps of glowing dots, Twin Peaks blinking, forever the vigil.

The apartment was stuffy, thick with the smell of dog. White fake antique furniture cluttered up the living room. Landscapes hung on the wall, horrid to the last.

"Would you like some music?"

I expected him to put on Montovani.

"Sure," Griffin said, looking at me, then scrunching up his face while the gent bent over his stereo.

"Ya got any Smashing Pumpkins?"

"What? Is that one of those rave groups?"

Griffin and I shared a chuckle, then I bravely betrayed my dopey hustler role and requested Ella.

"Oooh, a man of taste."

"Yeah, I got taste." I licked Griffin's face.

Griffin murmured, "C'mon, man, we gotta play it tough." I barely grinned, then switched to professional, and rude.

"The dog goes or we do," I glanced down at the sniveling, push-faced ottoman that nipped at my boots.

"Oh, well, I have a little cage for her. She hates it, but she will be out of the way."

"Good."

I pulled off my coat and slung it over a French Provincial chair. The gent disappeared with the mutt, and Griffin and I glanced at each other as we stripped.

"The decor," I whispered, sneering in over-exaggerated disgust. Griffin returned my glance with a cheerful malevolence. He pointed down, as if to say, here. We will soil his carpet. We will never even let him get us to the bedroom.

"Can I get you...a drink?" The gent returned to find us standing in the middle of his living room, both shirtless, necking. "Oh, I guess I'd better sit down and enjoy the show."

"Give us directions," I cued the man. He grinned.

"Strip each other," he instructed.

We did.

"Suck each other."

We did.

"Spank his ass."

I did.

"Fuck him."

I did.

The gentleman got in on the action, and I even tried to fuck him, but decided to ask if he had a dildo, which he had, one of those big veiny models. The guy's ass seemed more ready for that than my own average cock, and besides, it was a bit mushy in there, like screwing a cushion.

While shoving the dildo in and out of the gent's mushy ass, Griffin yanked him off, then the guy watched us go to work. I pounded into Griffin, and the man sat beside us on the carpet, sipping his drink, clutching his penis.

At the last moment, I ripped my cock out of Griffin, making him gasp. A bit of shit clung to the tip of the rubber. I snapped it off, then flung it behind me.

"Give me your glass."

"I can make you a drink," the gent said, suddenly not trusting me.

"The glass."

I shoved Griffin down as he rolled over on his back, yanking his cock. I took the man's drink and shoved my cock down into it, the ice cooling the head of my cock, but not before I squirted into the bourbon, veered the glass toward the man, who almost took it.

In a swift arc, I tossed the drink down, swallowing the liquids. I lowered my lips to Griffin's belly, spitting the ice onto his torso. He cringed, trying to wiggle away, but his gasps combined with his slick pumping noises, and he shot over the side of my face.

I sat up and crunched the ice while he licked his come off my ear and chin.

The man offered us money. $240. Nice tip. We kissed him goodnight after we dressed. He gave us his phone number, a little card with his name and number, and a dopey graphic of an antique chair.

Once on the street, I gave it to Griffin, and as we reached my bike, he sang a bit of a familiar song I couldn't place, "Just another sad old man, all alone dying of cancer…" and crumpled the card, tossing it into the street.

"I've discovered, for instance, that people are frightened that I'm going to write about them if we have sex, and they can't get past the idea that perhaps I'm taking notes when we're in the bedroom."

– John Preston

13

"Have you ever done S and M stuff?" he asked with a wicked twinkle in his eyes.

We were getting dressed to go to the Eagle for a beer bust. Griffin and I both decided to wear two little dog chains around our necks. We'd smoked joints after a shower, and dressed slowly, tossing leather and jeans and boots all over the place.

"Yeah, I've done it."

"Like what?"

"Like getting tied up. Like smacking around. Like scenes."

"Good. Then you know what to do."

"I guess you could call me...experienced." I grazed my palm over his back, imagining his arms tied behind him, immobile, victim of my drawn out desires.

We rode down to SoMa, and as I locked Rose, I asked him if he wanted to trade keys, just as a joke.

"Nobody gets the key to my collar."

"Really?"

"Yeah."

"Well, that's good to know," I said, burning inside, like I'd broached a too-touchy zone for him.

We entered Eagle-land, feeling good and safe, knowing anyone who bugged us would get more than they expected. I liked that about walking with Griffin, the power of knowing if we got attacked, he would whale into whoever tried it. That power, that compatriot timbre of potential violence, I liked.

I suspected he wanted to bring in a real third this time, like he kept pushing my boundaries, daring, a kid on a field trip playing with fire, learning to shoot rabbits. We went to the men's room and unzipped next to each other. He grabbed my cock as I started to piss, then I did the same with him. We were comfortable with it, and only getting half hard, so we could still piss when a handsome older guy came up to us, unzipped his jeans to haul out a very large cock, and began pissing beside us, watching our cocks in the convenient hip level mirror on the wall above the trough.

But I didn't make a move, and neither did Griffin, so we left the guy in his amusement, since four others were waiting in line behind us.

"So, ya wanna?" Griffin was back to the bondage scene proposal. We were on our third cup of poured pitcher beer, and I wanted to piss again, but somewhere else.

I wondered how to respond. Would he be like the others, the ones who craved my potential for intensity, only to cringe from its glow in the morning light? Would they be able to eat breakfast with a man who'd bound them, loved them with a punch fuck and a twist of flesh?

"Sure, we could do that," I said. "But I'm a bit fucked up right now."

"When you lose control, you'll reap the harvest you've sown."

"What is that from?" I asked, but he changed the topic back to sex.

"No, we'll do a major scene. Next time."

But with those two words, Griffin was teasing me, tormenting me, and finally releasing me with the gift of it all, the possibility of a next time. He didn't ever realize that that was what held me so, ropes or none. He held the ropes, the potential for my pain, which he could induce, and would, with a mere "goodbye."

I wanted to walk off the beer buzz before straddling my bike, so Griffin and I sauntered across the Eagle under the highway, where we admired a few Mack trucks parked in a fenced lot.

"Sure. Let's do it," I said.

"Okay. Um, you better not have any plans for the next day."

"Well, you might be too sore to work, and well, it may take a while. Hey look." The gate to the fenced parking lot was unlocked. "I gotta piss again. C'mon."

We both took a nervous glance, then snuck into the parking lot, where behind a truck, we unzipped. I saw Griffin reach a hand up, just to feel the cold girth of the machines, and as our streams unleashed a bit of steam, he passed his hand through it like a kid playing in the beam of a flashlight.

Before the last droplets fell to the ground, I was hard, and his mouth was wrapping around my cock. I let him go at it, carefully watching in both directions, knowing we could be seen by just the very careful darting eye of speeding drivers or passengers under the highway, each too rushed to stop and interfere, but seeing us just long enough to think, "No, it couldn't be." I was nearly coming, so I wrenched his face from my cock.

"So, we gonna do it?" I asked.

"Sure."

"Right. Friday."

"Eight."

"Okay."

"Okay what?" I slapped his cheek with my wet dick.

"Huh?" His hand went for my cock. I batted it away.

"Okay what, dog?"

"Oh, okay...sir."

I smiled, knowing he would please me, and I him, for when he brought me close, after licking some more, and sucking, I knelt before him, and then he sat on the step of the cab, and I sucked, and we both shot on the tires of that big rig, hoping to give that trucker a boner just from the stains that he would find.

14

Since I figured the neighbors shouldn't hear our noises and moaning, I made a special mix tape, to be played loud. None of that disco Crisco shit; metal, grunge and water-based lube.

I unplugged the phone, erasing Harlan and Denton's backlog of unanswered messages. I hadn't seen either of them in weeks. They weren't a part of this new world whose population was me and Griff. Everyone else was alien.

When he entered, I decided to start in right away, just to get his goat.

The lights were low, candles only. I was in black jeans and a white T-shirt. Bare feet. No cliché leather this time.

I had him strip at the bottom of the stairs and drop his clothes at the foyer, then he stood naked at the bottom of the stairs.

"Come to me," I said. He started bounding up the stairs. I could have enjoyed the sight, his cock wagging back and forth, but I wanted to give him more.

"On all fours."

He stopped, checking me, then grinned, as if he knew it was all just a game.

When he got to the stairs, I collared him.

"Pick a safe word," I whispered. I saw him considering, thinking, and surveying the apartment. No chains, no gauntlets, nothing obscene lay waiting.

He looked at me and said, "Thomas." My Christian name. Even in our little power play, he threw back at me what was myself.

I spat in his face.

He licked it, opened his mouth, wanting more.

Thus it began, our great night of "torture," or at least the outward actions of what would continue in our affair.

Neither of us really cared for the taste of shoe polish, so I merely had him lick my clean feet, sucking each toe, swirling the little hairs on my toe knuckles with his tongue. He tickled the underside, rubbed his face along my ankles, massaged me. He was a good boy.

Once I'd gotten the mattress down on the floor, at the base of the fireplace, I knew he'd figured out how I would bind him. He returned from the bathroom, cleaning out his ass, I could tell from the rude toilet sounds. He saw the candles laid out, the music starting, the mattress, and the bundle of rope.

"Huh, you finally figured out how to really use that fucking shrine."

"Yes, the Fucking Shrine. Care to lie?"

"No, the truth. Beat it out of me." He lay down before me, comfortable, coy, like a cat, waiting for the boot to come up and shove him down. but I waited.

"The columns are just wood, so don't get too dramatic."

"Don't fuck me too hard and I won't." He coiled himself around my leg, and I felt the warmth surge up through me, up my legs to my groin.

I didn't have fancy riding crops or flashy toys. I didn't have the budget or the interest in all that Betty Crocker goes Noir crap. I used my hands to smack his ass. I used my own belt to whip him. I used my own feet to shove on top of him. The thought of punishing him seemed silly, but after a while, I got into it, especially when he quivered or grunted just so. Blindfolding him with an old Cub Scouts kerchief helped. I knew he was still Griffin, but he didn't know where it was coming from. The flinches stirred me, as if his whole body were the sexual organ, and my ministrations building him up to more than what his roped-up cock could spit out.

The idea of pain and suffering on his part became easier. Perhaps I was torturing him in advance for all the suffering he would later cause.

I wasn't going to deprive him of real sex, though. I'd had the view of his exposed ass too long, and draped my stiff dick across all regions of his body too much not to fuck.

A spare shoe string served well to bind his erection. I criss-crossed it, thinking of Robin Hood leggings or gladiator's sandals. The string neatly ended after a loop around the base of his cockhead, and I yanked it a few times. He grunted a sort "unm-hmm."

"You like that, huh?" I muttered. He nodded. I yanked the cord up, pulling his cock until his hips rose. I held him like that a while, until his cock head turned a shade of violet.

I took a surgical glove and gooped his clean hole for a long time, massaging, poking, shoving slow as molasses, then spreading each side, opening it for me and only me.

I'd always wanted to know what that felt like, to plunge into an ass cockhead first, no mercy, so I did it. Good thing he was gagged.

I slammed into his ass, a wide open plain of male pussy. He took it in, and gulped occasionally, choking on the gag, or making choking noises, just to pretend, to feel the thought of bondage, of getting what you cannot bear, of getting fucked without a rubber.

We thought about that. We pretended we didn't care if we died fucking each other, but we didn't do it, because I wanted to think about doing it like this as old men, with mustaches and a house, and still treating each other like total trash once a full moon or so.

I leaned back, took a big long breath, as if sucking on a cigarette, and let the air come in, shifting. I felt the blood recede from my cock a bit, and I softened slightly. But his ass ring clenched like those anemones on the rocks, winking around my tool, and I couldn't help giving his ass another shove, half a shove, just to remind him that, other than my thighs under his backbone, it was all that touched him.

I closed my eyes, for once not even worrying if I was pleasing him, and thought of years of dreams, dark, dank reflections of locker room mazes, semi-naked boys, taunting me, thrilling me to small panic, and I thought of reaching into those dreams, and grabbing every one of those big muscley football boys and lanky boned tracksters and hairy coaches and I fucked the come out of every single one of them, one after one, and I tore out of that maze and opened the door and under me lay Griffin and I ripped off his gag and stuck my mouth on him while he panted up into me. I shucked the blindfold up over his head and grabbed his face. Our eyes were out-of-focus close. I bit his neck and shot up into him. Our bellies bashed against each other and his cock rubbed up into my navel and got gooey. We stuck.

His legs creaked like a rusty lawn chair. Slowly, I eased him down and watched his belly rise and fall with heaving breaths, giggles and pants, sighs of collapse. Our bodies were as rubble.

"Oh, man, I am spent."

"You know, it's gonna get harder as you get older."

"What, fucking?"

"Everything."

I glared at him. "I don't recall giving you permission to speak." But then he laughed, right out loud, as if to say, this whole thing is a joke. You will never own me. We will never own each other.

Somehow, I found the energy in my queasy legs to get him a glass of water. He shrugged off the towel.

"I want to smell it as it dries on me."

"I wish I could lick it off."

"This one guy told me if you let it out in the air, the virus dies. It's actually quite unstable."

"And we're both negative anyway..." one of us said, each of us half-believing it.

"And we didn't brush our teeth..."

We found more and more excuses as slowly, dangerously, we licked our own puddles, and I licked the taste of him in his mouth, and his pits, and couldn't help but feel like we'd crossed some border, into the land of fools, hazy and intoxicated with stupid desire.

15

We'd spent about four days apart, not calling, just waiting each other out. Who would crave first?

I was at A Different Light and picked up a few flyers, out of curiosity. Glossy, swirly nightclub invites, lesbian sewing circles, and also, with a picture of a half-nude Etienne in a sailor cap, his cock arcing out like a fire hose, an invite for Uniform Night at The Cock Factory.

I got hard just thinking about it.

I'd go with Griffin.

After returning from lunch, I had a voicemail message from seven people, including Griffin. I called him first, parking my feet up on my desk, even though my editors walked by, like, shouldn't you be doing something?

"How's the lovely world of work?" he asked.

"Hell with a paycheck."

"Told what to do by the man."

"Huh?"

"What's up?"

"Oh, uh, I thought we'd have another little adventure." He seemed intrigued, so I explained it to him, all the time getting a slight boner. People walked by my desk. I rearranged the growing mound in my crotch and spoke softly.

"Do you have two uniforms?" he asked.

"I got a P-coat, which I've worn on many a night to such a place. I've got a sailor cap and dress pants. I'll wear a white T-shirt and dog tags. My Doccies aren't uniform regulation, but they'll do."

"I'm getting hard." he said.

So was I. An editor ambled by. I smiled.

"What am I gonna wear?"

"Um, whaddaya got?"

"Fatigue pants."

"Long as it's not that awful Desert Storm drag, I'm sure you'll look great."

"Aww, those were so stupid."

"Yeah, well, the uniforms weren't the only thing stupid. How 'bout strafing a highway of fleeing civilians until they were brown as toast–"

"You're so hot when you get political."

"Shut up," I scorned him to silence. I could never tell when he was being sarcastic, or real, or both.

We made plans to meet at my place, since I had more stuff from a quick Army-Navy shopping binge, and Griffin showed up a little late, like five minutes.

Punctuality is not only good manners, it works wonders on the heart, relieving the "Gee, does he...?" pangs at the window, replacing them with a sure, solid feeling, like trust, and it's below your belt sometimes. Cock logic.

By the time we finished raiding the refrigerator for last minute carbs, and brushing our teeth and packing about a dozen rubbers, we were dressed and ready.

Then he said, "C'mere," and took me up on the bed, standing. I don't have any mirrors in my home, except the medicine cabinet, and the fireplace mantle, the shrine. To see my own cock on lonely nights, or just to see how my outfit looks, I have to stand on the bed.

Well, that position, with Griffin, and the music still on, and the lights low, and us in uniforms, it was like *Big Guns* times six.

We didn't kiss at first.

We watched each other fish a dick out of the pants across from us, yank and then smooch, stumble, and fall to the bed, crotch to crotch, peeling off the uniforms, like green and black husks, and getting down to chomping, slurping, and generally invading each other's groin with fingers and tongues.

It got to the point where I was pumping down into Griffin's mouth, going down on him the easy way, cock bent back, and slick, and flipping by that gag muscle with ease. We were just about ready to start grunting, the goo backing up for a blast, when I pulled off him with a smack, stood to get a rubber out of whatever pocket.

But he wouldn't stop. He sat up, lapping on my dangling balls, until I slammed my boner back into him, then, since his blow job technique chafed a bit in that position, I pulled back, until he got it, just slurping the head like a big juicy lipstick.

"Yah, just kiss it."

"Mnnn," he purred, then sort of gurgled a glob of spit.

"Welcome what is about to relocate." I slipped the rubber on, grabbed for the goop and shoved Griffin back, his legs floating high. I grabbed him by the pants and slipped under, his uniform wrapped around his ankles like a sturdy knot.

"Man, shit," he hooted as I shoved a finger in, then about, then plowed in, ultra major homo slomo.

It wasn't more than a few minutes before I was banging away, sliding my meat in and out in low thrusts, occasionally revving up, that he shot, and I thought, awww, oh well.

But after a bit of his taut belly quivering as it turned into a sperm Danish, he shoved my still hard bone out of his ass, pushed me down onto the floor, and grabbed one of the tossed out unused rubbers that fell out of my pocket sometime mid-fuck.

He wasn't nearly as polite, and started pounding a bit too fast for my colon.

But I weathered his jabs, and clutched my cap.

The hat ended up below my eyes, and suddenly, we were anonymous to each other, me every Navy boy in my imagination getting plowed, South Specific, up my ass, and my cock was flapping up and down on my belly like a just-splayed tuna, flapping around on deck for the last gasps. I refused to touch it, just let him bang the come up and outta me.

He really did, but politely pulled out to truly jack my cock. Half his hand had replaced his cock, nestled up me, teasing now, while his mouth gamboled my balls around like a cupped hand rolling dice.

My sperm dribbled out at first, one runny one, and then the big first blast spat him on the chin. The next glob jumped up but splashed back down onto his thumb, that ridge between it and the index, which, with its three brothers, choked more globs of come out of my dick.

I was about to lean up and lick the come off his face, when he reached back and ran the jizz on his hand though his hair.

"Suck it out," he said, and leaned down over me. It was like sesame noodles, only sweet.

I lay back, eyes closed, my arm over his chest, and felt his heartbeat thumping through his ribs. I started to doze, but he nudged me, "C'mon, gotta stay awake." He was up.

"Why?"

"Let's go," he said and then jumped out of the bed in a sort of yelp of a laugh.

I burst out chuckling at the ridiculous idea of going out to have sex when we'd already had sex, but then we just kept putting our pants back on, and then I was getting the keys and he was grabbing more rubbers and we were putting our coats and helmets on and tooling down to SoMa.

But by the time we got to the sex club, we thought that sex itself was just too little, and since we only occasionally parted, I guess we were a little threatening.

We did find one brave boy who happened to be kneeling already. He took our dicks, one, then the other, and then both, quite a feat. I'd always wondered what that felt like.

We had no intentions of shooting, but this was a great warm-up. A few other guys came by to watch, and one didn't waste more than a half a minute before he unpeeled his too-tight jeans and started twisting and gripping his too-long cock.

The guy would have come on us, but he got his own dick boy, and watched, occasionally glancing up from the lover between his legs. Somebody ejaculated, because I heard some grunting and felt something wet hit my pants, and I guess it was the boy, cause the daddy just sidled over and tried to make a "three dicks in the fountain" formation.

But it got a little crowded. We would have persisted, but then the dad pulled out a bottle of poppers, and just the smell, I mean, that was enough to dredge up every dead casualty from AIDS, every Village People disco ghost, and both our cocks just sort of went, "Oh man."

So we guided the guy into a more accessible position for our suck boy, whose crewcut head still chafed my palm.

We went out onto the main floor, and kind of found a nice little pool of narcissistic light, amber with a key in dark aqua.

We started dancing, just to shake it up, freak out that turnstile of ridiculous sad flesh. Maybe it was just that it was a deep remix of "In Your Room," Depeche Mode. Public/Private.

We humped with the uniforms on, grinding, and getting hard. Since we'd been fucking already, his lube juices still moist in my ass, all it took was another little poke, and each of us, with a hand down shorts, a finger up each other's bung, and a hand on each other's cock, our tongued slurping, entwined, and we blasted, whiledancing.

Minutes, or hours, passed. I don't remember.

Like me, Griffin leaned back, way back, and let the fountain bring the other guys into a grin at least, if not ejaculation. The crowd varied, but that's what we liked about it, as we wiped off in the john and each pissed into one guy's mouth, some little troll who seemed to live there.

"Whew! That was fun," Griffin said.

We glanced down, arms back, wiping the sweat off each other's backs. I licked it up, of course, a salty tequila.

Finished pissing, we patted the gent on the head and buttoned up. Griffin helped me with my nearly impossible sailor buttons, tucking my cock back inside the flap, while some guy just stared at us. Querelle goes backstage or something.

During the ride home, I thought of Brad Davis, and the time I'd met him. It was an ACT UP benefit performance of *The Normal Heart*. Shaking hands with him, years before he died, was a high point of my New York days.

You think it a digression, this "brush with fame," but I merely offer it as an example of the roles we play, or our lovers play, when we truly get off. How many times had I traced the image of Davis, in *Midnight Express,* and *Querelle,* while beating my meat on lonely nights? What is deep down there in the spurt Rolodex that hits our buttons? That older brother in *Flipper*? Don Robinson? Huey Lewis?

With Griffin, I never thought of anyone but him. He was all those guys, like a CD ROM flipcard of memories, but then he would laugh, or pull out, or bite me too hard, the channel changed.

Was such good sex showing love, or merely good technique? Either way, I was enjoying the ride.

What we didn't enjoy until we got home was a good shower. With Griffin, I wanted an exalted shower, ten spouts in a row, a swim team lined up and giddy after finals.

Instead, we took a bath after riding home in the sloppy rain, our feet becoming puddled in the soup of our stripped-off clothes, which were sweaty and stained and wet from the road, so we just dropped them in the tub water, rinsed off, and soaped each other down, Cadmus boys after the gogo.

Hanging our dripping clothes up on the cramped back porch, I left the tub full. After he left in the morning, I dunked myself into it, shivering cold, jolted awake for a day of remembering.

16

At the height of it, when I was edgily, softly saying "boyfriend" to a few people about Griffin, but not to Griffin, Lee invited us to his drag party. We went shopping together at Piedmont, a crowded drag store on Upper Haight. Griffin seemed thrilled to get gussied up in fishnets.

The night of the party, I carefully timed the calling, and eventual, if not interminable, await for our cab. I was not riding Rose in heels and a miniskirt.

Griffin made jokes when I dressed so quickly and easily, transforming myself into a cross between Siouxsie (of the Banshees) and my Aunt Beulah.

He had settled on a black body suit with fake fur puffed around the neck, black fishnets and boots.

"Goth Chihuahua," I joked.

"You. Look at you."

"What's my new drag name?"

"Formica Topping."

"I think that's taken."

"Yeah, well, I'm gonna be ready for some taking, ho." He nudged his crotch up under my skirt, and muttered, as he pawed my bean bags, "Maybe I'm gonna fuck a girl tonight."

"Or get fucked by one," I said to the mirror. I saw his gaze, and tried to remember how long it had been since that first time when I shoved my cock in him, and saw our eyes meet in the mirror, but with me behind. Griffin's eyes twinkled, reveling in the prospect of perversity as sport, as dare.

The cab driver didn't even flinch as we awkwardly poured ourselves into his car. We ended up joking a lot with him, though, while he joked about not being able to decide whether we were sexier as girls or guys. That's what I loved about San Francisco. Most people are easy-going about any sort of choice like that. We still seemed to need to assure him that this wasn't our usual thing, but we were having fun, except for those damn heels.

We arrived in a grand entrance, Griffin having gotten down on all fours, me fastening the leash to his collar. The girlish shrieks filled the apartment, and bouncing disco music kept spirits truly gay.

Lee entered under four feet of hair with little silk butterflies attached to his whirling dervish of hair.

It came the time for the 'performance,' and Lee and a few others lip-synched to some show tunes. A couple of them were professional dancers, and despite their wigs flinging off a few times, they socked it to us, leaving us hooting and hollering for more.

Griffin and I danced, and Lee snapped a flash shot of us for posterity. We humped and bumped, and Griffin edged his hand up my thigh to the trapped contents at the crotch of my panty hose.

I never felt so faux-sexy, like it was all an act. He kissed me, but I shoved him away.

"You'll ruin my lips," I hissed, and instead we hugged and held hands while other queens, bound into one outrageous costume or another, whirled about the living room, sashaying and runwaying.

But the joy seemed to have faded especially quick when I saw myself in the bathroom mirror, a sweaty, tarted corpse of a woman, a travesty. I suddenly feared that Griffin's seeing me like this would forever hinder the charms of the real me, the masculine boy man, the me I had spent so many years impersonating.

"C'mon, kid, this bra's killin' me. Let's close this show."

Stripping off the drag with the speed of showgirls between numbers, we both assumed that the prospect of remaining bound up in that stuff eliminated the potential kink of sex in it.

We lay in bed, our skin expanding into a comfortable pair of catcher's pitcher's gloves.

"I can't wait to see the pictures," I said softly. "I'm gonna send one to my mom."

"Your mother?" Griffin said.

"Sure, why not? She'll probably get a real kick out of it, put it on the refrigerator."

"Your parents must be really cool."

"They try."

"Mine would f_p," he said.

"Where is it you're from again?"

"Well, all over. I was born in Nebraska, but my mom got divorced and then we lived in Fresno."

"Isn't there a prison there?"

"Yeah, it's called My Home."

"Huh."

I rubbed his back, and we slid a little from under the covers. I wanted sex, but he seemed too tired.

And then, in that exhausted state, he rambled out a story, and I knew he was finally trusting me, for it revealed more about his needs than I think he knew.

"My parents were awful. Always awful. Drinkin', fighting. White trash. I was born in a house full of pain. It didn't get any better when they got divorced, 'cause I had to see him sometimes, too. He used to beat me, do things to me. It was not like in those *Straight To Hell* stories you read to me, let me tell you. I hated him almost as much as my mother, and she was a mess. Baptists. Huh, jus' goes to show what a religious upbringing'll do to fuck ya up."

I was as exhausted as he, touched by his confession, but couldn't think of anything but caressing him. He lay on the bed, ready for sleep. I left the shades open just a sliver, and pulled the covers up around us, placed my arm gently over him, and lay next to him, my hardon just bumping his butt. He didn't respond. I didn't relent.

I waited, until his breath slowed, as did mine, but my hardon, and my desire, refused sleep. I grazed his back with my fingers, and he rolled over onto his stomach.

I pulled the covers down slightly. It wasn't cold, and he didn't seem to mind. I eased my head over him slowly, and began lightly grazing my lips over his back, down his spine, over to his lats, grazing, never wet and leech-like, just grazing, feeling the warmth emanate from his skin.

And then I went lower. My face was drawn to the rise of his buttocks, and my hands delicately held the two globes that I'd caressed, licked, smacked until they were red. But this time, as if he were a delicate butterfly specimen, where one touch could crumble its fragile colored dust, I went lower, between his mounds of flesh, into his ass, just grazing my nose into him, barely touching. He smelled clean, with just a trace of human funk, and I brought one hand to my cock. In a mere few tugs, I brought myself to bursting, spilling over his thigh, onto the sheet, into my hand, quivering with a pathetic gesture, his unknowing, or uncaring as I tingled from his mere presence. It was then that we both knew who controlled this love, who held the reins, and it scared me as I licked the remnants of my desire, savoring its commingling with my spit on his leg hairs.

I drew back up, lay down and rolled over, back to him, scared, humiliated, feverish, and slept, not touching him.

I dreamt of the hill on Bernal Heights, looming. I was flying low, as if on my bike, but the bike was nowhere. Nothing was under me but moving air, and the road was abandoned, but the hill stayed just on the horizon, never coming closer, always in the near distance.

17

We had done everything, it seemed, at least everything within the boundaries of our taste, our limits, our desires. There would be no mind fucks, no blood-letting. We were too enamored of each other's bodies to offer such a serious sacrifice. The thought of hurting him in that way made my stomach quiver. We never had a "session" of BDSM again. But there was one thing we had joked about, hinted at, but had never done.

In the bathroom, in the mornings, or at night, after sex, when we couldn't stand being away for a few minutes between humping and sleeping, we often pissed together, standing at the toilet, watching, giggling, crossing streams, feeling the release of that simple bodily function, often with boners that wouldn't yet go down, ignoring the fact that we remained hard because we watched each other piss.

It was a day, a full moon day, when we did it, a Sunday, another beer bust. We had thought of dressing in leathers, but mutually scoffed at the idea, as if it were the dress code of a costume ball, and it was, and we were determined to break the rules.

We held hands as we wove through the packed crowd at the Eagle. We shared a cup after making the ten-dollar donation, and drank freely of the cold yellow brew, poured out in pitchers by young and older men in singlets. I greeted a few of the wrestling team members, told one I was from New York, and had met a few grapplers in my hunt for a man worthy of my energies. One of them had proven more than worthy.

It warmed me to introduce Griffin to the men I knew, and to brush past the bellies of older men, their smiles spreading as we pinched nipples and received friendly butt pats.

We kissed and drank, drank and giggled, as a burly little white-haired MC rambled on at the microphone. Our bladders filled to an almost painful state, yet we only once escaped to the cock-comparing toilet, sidling up on either side of a tall daddy, who let loose a thick stream of piss, stroking his thick soft cock for our enjoyment. I saw Griffin lick his lips in mock horniness, and we finished, heading off together.

I said, "Let's walk. I'm too drunk."

"Aw, yeah, let's piss in an alley."

"No. We wait until home."

He didn't speak much. Neither did I. Either our bowels hurt too much, or the anticipation scared us.

But that all dissolved as the door keys jingled us into privacy, and we began a drunken kiss that ended with our fumbling for our clothes.

We ended up standing at the toilet, then I shoved him over to the bathtub, and we aimed downward. I reached over to his cock and felt the buzzing movement in his penis as his piss gushed forth. Then I knelt down, and he pushed me into the tub. The stream hit my shoulder. I remember that first warm splash. I knelt down in the tub, and he arced his stream all over my body as I crouched, enamored, entranced by the release.

He halted his stream and stepped in with me, pushed me to standing, and knelt, mouth open. I teased him by pissing in his hair, then down to his chest, avoiding his mouth, then finally aiming to his laid out tongue, where he lapped at it, hungrily, growling.

We were drunk, and I halted my flow, so it became as a dozen small ejaculations of liquid.

Unlike our sperm, this we could drink and savor with some greater level of safety, and the beer piss, clear and hot and endless, it seemed, served as the hundreds of spermy ejaculations the plague had denied us.

I knelt then, and opened my mouth, and he fitted his cock into my mouth like the comfortable slot it was. I let his piss pool in my mouth, and gulped, squinting my eyes from the warm sting of it. I gargled in it, and we both crept down on the tub's floor, pissing on each other, close, like humping boys, shivering from the excess of it, that and the cold porcelain of the tub.

We gasped and burped and laughed at the sordid excess of it, and I turned on the shower, our cheap lust washed away in favor of more cleanly activities.

We soaped up and jacked off, and I reached over to the cabinet and found a rubber and some lube, and he fucked me standing, the water pouring down on us.

I don't know if he shot, I didn't care. It was my turn, and my cock was stiff as a morning piss hard.

I thrust into him, and he gripped the edges of the tub, and I slapped his ass, and drove in and out, and fumbled and slipped out.

And drove in again, and came up his ass, reaching around, seeing that no, he hadn't come, or had come again, in my hands.

Oh, and one of the neighbors banged on a wall a few times.

We stopped.

"Sheez, were we that loud?"

I shrugged.

The clots of come refused to come off his pubes, and I scrubbed it off, the sad little bits of glue, and we dried off, and hopped to the bed, and we slept the rest of the drunken day away, until evening came, and we were hungry.

We wolfed down spaghetti, and licked the sauce off each other's faces. I looked away, and he took my chin in his hand and dared me to stare at him, into his sharp glare, burning away the embarrassment of my lust. He defied guilt, defied shame. He refused it.

With almost all other men in my life, when the first night of incredible passion continued on to dating and going out, forcing each other on our friends for approval, there was a distance after a while, a sort of settling into a bored domesticity.

The idea of going out to do something, a movie, a play, became merely a ruse for the eventual, then declining, sex. Finally, the sexual connection dwindled, like a poorly watered plant, and then the thing died. Phone calls became disparate, then nothing, then hapless encounters and false kisses at parties and cafes.

With Griffin, the intensity of our sex and our getting to know each other only increased, until our lovemaking became feverish, sometimes comic, but always intense. Once, when he forced me to the brink of ejaculation, then slathered my seed over his face, grabbing my head and forcing me to lick it off, I felt as if I were being force-fed that which he had gleefully drained of me. It wasn't just sperm. It was white blood.

And then he disappeared for a week, a long tortuous week, where I desperately wanted to leave a message, yet I tested myself, knowing he would return from the mysterious mission he was on. But then the jealous flares rose up, and I imagined him in the arms of another, laughing to himself, as I knew he would, seeing me, as if through buildings and across the city's loping hillsides, seeing into my home, me, huddled alone, waiting for only him.

The days were painful, nights restless, full of imagined accidents and betrayals. Friday, after a week of his complete absence, without a word, and that surly het roommate just grunting, lying, saying he would leave a message, toying with me, I took the day off, got extra stoned, and in my cloud, my paranoid cloud, I called, leaving a message, the message I will regret for the end of my days. I curse the phone machine, the horrible mechanism that slices out a bit of our souls with every high-pitched beep. The barrier. The electronic wall.

Something about "Look, if this is your way of breaking up with me, it's not gonna work. I don't go away that easy. You are not gonna give yourself to someone else after all we've been through. You will not escape me. I will haunt you."

Dacryphiliac:
Someone who gets
sexually aroused from
watching other people cry.

18

Anxious, thinking I might bump into him in the Castro, a ridiculous thought, since he rarely went there, I rode up Market, fooling myself into thinking I was just shopping.

I was on the corner of Market, 16th and Noe, that ridiculous six-way intersection where a hundred car crashes are narrowly avoided each hour. Queers of all shapes and sizes strolled past with their usual glazed-over absent looks, stopping to chat with friends, ignoring others. A huge blanket of fog was creeping its way over Twin Peaks, looming like a monster.

"Hey, hot!"

It was Bobbie Bubble, handing out club invites while sitting on a news rack. A couple of waifs were standing near him as he basked in his celebutantitude. I took one of the invites, and bid the ebullient devil good day.

"So, where's the boy?" Bobbie gushed.

"Huh? Oh, Griffin."

"Who else?"

"Well, you know, we're not like, living together or anything. I'm probably gonna see him this weekend."

"For the whole weekend. Tie him up, tie him down!" He laughed loudly, like a clown at the circus who has something nasty to show you behind his tent. "I never took you for that type of guy," he said, leading me in.

"What kind of guy?"

"Oh, you know, the bondage thing. You must have seen his videos! And he used to be, or still is, a slave to some old guy in the 'burbs. Told me this one night. He was so drunk, gogo dancing on the bar, oh man, you have lassoed yourself one wild little—"

It is amazing that Bobbie forgave me, months afterward, when the scene sucked it up as just another little event to be chewed over the gossip tongues and latte-smeared lips, then burped out and discarded for some other *scandale petit,* but I do remember, after shoving him off the news rack with one hand, still smiling dumbly, as he fell ass backward, the slight fluttering sound the club invites made as they flew up, like a small flock of birds, then landed down on the sidewalk around him.

At home, I waited.

I knew I could find any videos he made at one of a dozen gay porn shops.

It was as if I had assaulted myself, and couldn't punish the criminal.

Videos?

When he finally called, it was as bad as I thought. I was wrong, or not, or nothing, or something. He said he was out of town, like he'd told me. Like I'd listened.

"I didn't know where you were," I said. "I thought... I mean, we were together all those days and then nothing."

"I told you I was going out of town."

"Where?"

"To visit a friend."

"The master?"

"What?"

"I know all about it."

"About what?"

"The dungeon. The money. The man who ties you up and does all the things to you that if I was that twisted I'd do to you, just to keep you, but I can't..."

"That is none of your business."

"But you see, it is, Griff. You're part of my life now, a big part, and you can't just do these things..."

"I'll do whatever the fuck I want."

"How can you do whatever you want when you're locked in a cage with a chain around your neck? Huh? Tell me that."

"You don't understand. It's a very different thing."

"Different? It's different, all right."

"I mean, jeezus, If I'd known you were gonna get all psycho on me like that I would have left you a long time ago. 'I will haunt you?'"

"I'm sorry. I didn't know what I was saying."

"That was so upsetting."

Silence

I spoke. "I'll understand if you never want to see me again. I'll understand. But I will never forgive myself."

"Look, you're gonna have to calm down and just think about things. I don't think we should see each other for a while."

"Fine. I understand."

"So don't go doing anything stupid."

"No, I just need some time."

"What are you gonna do?"

"I think I'll just go to ocean and think a while, drown my sorrows."

"Well, have a good drown."

131

Some people hinted at it. Harlan did, since he'd tried it once. Denton and Vic were, well, polite, and they visited me in the hospital, too.

Guess who didn't?

It really was an accident. I gave up trying to convince everyone of that soon enough.

I was riding, just riding, out in the mountains, above Daly City, when it happened. I wasn't thinking about the turns, just trying to coast on them, exactly the sort of thing you're not supposed to do, but it felt good, for a time.

Then I started thinking about him and got distracted. That's what I tell myself.

The bike just slid out from under me.

I rolled with it, the weight crunching down on the asphalt beside me, then above me, then way off somewhere, and I just could not stop tumbling, hurtling, flying low off the ground. For a moment I felt totally weightless, hurled by the velocity, and I saw the basin of a city yawning out below me and a tree limb just came out of nowhere and cut me in half.

19

I woke up later with a shrub in my face.

The people that found me were nice. It seemed like a long time that I lay with a hand holding mine, the blood sort of blurring vision in my left eye. It seemed a day before I heard the ambulance, but the pain may have done that.

I spent three days in the hospital. A broken foot, contusions in about four places, and scrapes on all the major joints, only minor thanks to the leathers. Thank god I'd been wearing the road racing suit. Fuck what those complainers about helmet laws say. If I hadn't been wearing one, I would have defined the term Puddin Head. The Shoei was cracked like an egg.

The insurance was gonna pay for most of it, I later learned. There was an oil slick in the road, so it technically wasn't my fault, the guy said. Some guy in a tie. I had to fill out forms and more forms. In the meantime, I was sore, on disability, and laying around in bed, too weak to even think about Griffin or the fucking magazine.

Of course it was he that ended up haunting me. I could go on, describe the meeting on the street, the way he said he'd heard about my accident, but hadn't called. His saying so few words.

For days I'd lay in bed, then when I was feeling better, enough to go to work, I had to walk down to the bus stop. I was often late. Some days I just couldn't go out. But it's really too much to think about.

Suffice it to say that I was a mess, until one day, weeks later, Griffin called to invite me to his birthday party, as if nothing had ever gone wrong, as if I was just another of his friends, his collection.

It pained me to consider going, as much about seeing him amid perhaps dozens of others. Also, with Rose in the shop, banged up, I had to take the bus. The ride was lonely, but I figured I would leave him the same way, alone on a bus going home.

It was awkward, everything was awkward. What was worse was seeing Harlan there, and not even thinking to call him, or him call me, since I'd become such a depressive recluse.

He seemed embarrassed to see me, but eventually stayed nearby, chatting softly on the deck, where once I'd fucked Griffin in front of the whole world. I didn't tell Harlan that. I didn't say much. I was quite stunned to see a room full of twenty or so men and woman, and wonder who the hell these people were.

Some of them left, and others were putting together a group to go down to Fiend for some dancing. The beers were all gone anyway. My gift to Griffin, who had just entered chef's school, lay unopened. Inside was a monogrammed chef's jacket, with his lapel bearing his name. On either side, in Chinese characters, was his private nickname: BAD DOG.

But people were putting on coats, and music was being turned off, and I, like his retinue, was being herded out, moving the celebration of this boy-man out into the night.

Not being on my bike, I always felt out of control, like I had no choice in things, where I was going.

We rode in two cars, and I hid my disappointment when Griffin ended up in the other car. At least Harlan was by my side in one of Griffin's friends' back seat.

But that small joy I always got from having his warmth next to me was broken as he leaned over to me and whispered, soft, while the radio blasted and everyone else chatted away above it.

Harlan muttered into my ear, "Griffin made a pass at me in the bedroom."

"What?"

"I was alone with him for a minute, just chatting, and he just grabbed me and started kissing."

My response was blasé, a light crust over a burning pool of pain. "It's not like we're together again or anything."

That ended it, Harlan's glance in the dark light of the night. He put his arm protectively around me. For a brief moment I wondered if he were lying, just to ease my pain, bring me to a sense of reality. But he wouldn't have to. Griffin would have done such a thing. It was as if he thought he could keep all his sexual affairs and friends balanced on a platter, all of them merely there for his feeding.

I didn't mind going to Fiend with these strangers, this masquerade of unity, all of us bonded only by our relationship to Griffin.

I looked at the others as we huddled together outside the door, waiting to pay admission into the sweaty boxy room of slides and sound and jostling beer bottles.

I stood behind him, close enough to smell him, wanting to whisper, "Look, I'm being good. I'm being social. I'm sharing you, I'm being okay." I wanted to say something. Instead I bit him on the shoulder. He gave me an uncomprehending stare, then tried to laugh it off.

Once inside, Bauhaus blaring away, we got beers, Griffin at least deigned to buy me a Rolling Rock, but it wasn't more than a few minutes before he was on the dance floor with one of his friends, and Harlan and I were left adrift in the crowd of pierced tattooed goth kids, making dopey chit chat with a tall guy from the party, part of Griffin's collection. I couldn't even work up the nerve to ask how he knew Griff. I guzzled my beer and made my way up to him, preparing for a goodbye.

He danced low and close with his friend in a way I knew was too familiar for friends. I remembered trying that with Harlan years before at The Roxy, how abruptly he pulled away when our bumping hips, like soft magnets, were compelled to each other.

I watched Griffin dance, and remembered the nights I'd danced naked with him in our homes, the nights we'd shown off for others in nightclubs, the horizontal version of the dance, all blurring together as one tragic pool of joy gone mucky.

I watched his butt, his tight little back, the beginning of a sweat stain at the middle of his back, the closely shaved nape of his neck. I wanted to cut in, just like the old movies, but couldn't, wouldn't dare be so presumptuous.

Instead, I walked through the dance floor, stood behind him, leaned in and gave the back of his neck one last kiss, and shouted, "Happy Birthday. Goodbye."

As I turned, I felt tremors of a sick pleasure as he grabbed at me once, twice, and again, the last tugs of his desire. I felt a surge of pathetic strength as I ripped my arm away, hurtling through the crowd and off the dance floor, desperately hoping he'd follow, knowing he wouldn't, knowing I would not turn back.

I walked home, oblivious to any danger. I heard sirens and gunshots. All tragedy bounced around me like debris hitting a tiny cyclone.

Enclosed in my room, I pouted, trying not to peer out the window to see him come to me. I sat up for hours, then tried to sleep, but the pathetic mutterings and repeats of every moment with him, every joy and shard of pain, came back, haunting me, burning me. And then the tears came.

Half-awake, I heard the phone machine click on and the message that a friend of a friend, despondent over his increasing opportunistic infections, had sent off letters to a few friends, neatly taken care of his belongings and apartment, and dove off the Golden Gate Bridge.

I didn't react with shock, or pain. The pain had dulled. Misery had woven itself into my body like hair or skin.

I merely jostled myself lower under the covers, refusing to admit I was wakening, and brought my hand up to the fleshly part of my neck. Would a knife hurt a lot as it sliced my throat? How far would the blood spurt? Would I do it in the tub to keep things neat? But no, I wouldn't want to be found nude. I'd always imagined my corpse as less bluntly erotic, with jeans and boots on, at least. Wet with red blood in the tub, with jeans.

But growls of hunger moved my morbid thoughts to the day's needs, the simple cravings.

I called Harlan, and he didn't seem shocked at my revelations about suicide.

"I don't know anyone who hasn't tried it," he said. "Myself included."

"That says something about the world," I said.

"Or the company you keep."

While I waited for the insurance settlement to clear for me to get a new motorcycle, I bought a used bicycle. The doctor said it would be good therapy for my atrophied body. It hurt a little, but it felt good to me moving again, if not with a purring motor beneath me.

After a slew of rain that left me comfortably housebound, the sun came out for a while, and I went outside on a Monday holiday.

I rode around, feeling the soft thrill of wind rushing by, strangely quiet now without the purr of Rose under me, just the squeaking of gears. At least the wind was blowing through my hair through the foam helmet.

Parts of town were ruined for me, not just Fiend, but Duboce Park, where we ran through the sprinklers one night and jacked each other off on a bench.

Griffin barked after he came. I wanted very much to eat his come, but settled for my own. Being unsafe seemed a pathetic gesture of fealty, but could easily be interpreted as mere stupidity.

What saddened me so much was how little of me Griffin had taken the time to learn, "like he'd gone to Harvard on scholarship and had only taken wood shop," a poet said.

Griffin wouldn't really look at my designs, and after we got to a point of avoiding each other, I often wondered if Griffin had thrown out the drawing I'd given him, or if it hung over his bed like a hunting trophy.

I got home tired from the aimless riding, and took a hot bath. Eventually, the warm water and my nudity got me feeling good about my body again, and I started feeling myself up, soaping my cock and ass and chest, submerging in the wombed hum of being submerged in the water.

Then I decided to go a bit further, and douched out my ass, found the rubber dildo I'd stashed away in the closet. I remember thinking I'd never need that again with Griffin around, but felt glad that I'd saved it.

I won't say that my porno collection was exactly dust-covered from disuse, but it certainly was fun to get back to it after so long. It was like those pictures of cocks and asses and smiling men's faces, always ready, always muscled, some now dead, was still there, eager, and waiting, smiling, erect for all time. I settled my aching body down next to a small pile, and started pretending.

20

"You know, I just want to fall asleep with a man's cock in my mouth."

Harlan was a bit hyped after our little ACT UP demo. I'd ridden with him cramped in the back seat of a lesbian couple's hatchback. We had marched about some industrial park of some pharmaceutical company. I think we got the point across. Harlan and I kept cruising the truckers and construction workers. I don't know. It had none of the drama of ACT UP New York.

After it was over, I just kept enjoying him talking about these near-sex encounters with college chums. Harlan was a southerner. Lots of repression.

Of course, I had my share too, but that day, riding in the back seat, I just let him hold my hand. If he wouldn't have sex with me, the least I could do was enjoy his sex tales and at least have a boner in his presence.

We bid our two wimmin friends good day and had bad Chinese food for lunch at a place on Market Street. It was my birthday, so he paid.

"I don't even care if it's soft. I just want a cock in my mouth when I fall asleep. Can't do that anymore."

"Why not?"

"Well, you know, I have to be with guys who are positive or else I worry..."

"No, ya put a rubber on, pretend the extra latex is foreskin. You'll be snorin' like a baby, and he'd be spurtin' jizz real slow-like, you lick the third time around, where you don't even shoot, you just sort of ooze cum."

"You're way ahead of me."

"Ah, I wish."

"What else do you wish for?"

"I dunno." I didn't need a new bike. That was on its way.

"It's your birthday. What do you want to do?" Curl up beside him, or Griffin, once, or once more?

"I don't know, maybe go out for a beer. Whyncha call me later?"

"There's another underwear party tonight. I'd let you borrow my delectable little pair of Calvins. Wearing my underwear's almost like having sex with me," he giggled.

"The square-cut ones? Not the regulars?"

"You know what looks good on you!"

The waitress cleared our plates, silent yet smiling through our laughter. She set down fortune cookies.

Mine said, YOU WILL FIND LOVE AROUND THE CORNER.

Harlan's said, A LONG AND PROSPEROUS LIFE.

"Maybe if I cashed in on a viatical settlement," he sighed.

"That is, if you had life insurance."

We didn't laugh as hard at that.

"So, what else would you like, if you could have anything for your birthday?" Harlan's eyes seemed to glimmer, as if he could provide whatever my heart wished.

"What, besides you?"

"Come off it. We've been over that. You just want to mother me."

"I don't think you need a mother. I just want to take care of you, be with you..."

"Until I die?"

I said nothing.

"Doncha see?" Harlan said, as if he'd been telling me for years. Perhaps he had.

"You just want to be in love with me because you know I'm going to die. It fits your whole plan, that you refuse to allow yourself joy.

"You refuse to believe you can be happy, so you look for a loophole to make things go bad, and then you say, 'See, I didn't deserve it.' It's the same with Griffin."

"What?"

"You made the relationship fall apart because you couldn't stand being so happy."

"Like I couldn't stand him being a slut? Being totally undependable? Having to risk arrest just to have sex? Like that was something good?"

"Maybe you just wanted somebody wild, somebody to push your boundaries. I don't know. I do know that you could have at least made it last longer if you hadn't pressed the destruct button."

I toyed with the crumpled bits of fortune cookie, and looked around the restaurant. Happy couples, a few men, even a couple of women. Happy.

Harlan sounded like a self-help book, I knew that, but beyond the familiar-sounding lecture, I understood a bit. It reminded me of the time I'd seen *Forbidden Planet*, amazed at the special effects, never thinking as a kid about the corny moral.

"The Monster of the Id," I muttered.

"What? Are you losing it?"

"No, Harlan, I lost it. But maybe I won't let it happen again. Thanks."

"Okay, I think."

"C'mon. Let's get out of here."

I took my fortune and stuffed it in my pocket. "Now how about that Underwear Party?"

I didn't think I'd see him there, but it happened. I kept turning away as we danced, each of us keeping a distance.

Fucker. Bastard. Whore. Slut. I still loved him.

He seemed bigger, even from a distance. I imagined him at his gym, working out every other day or so. People would never be impressed by our muscles. It was our grace, and thin tautness, and the glow in our eyes, the ease with which a simple playful hip thrust while dancing at a party could evoke a wave of sexual desire in observers. We were both lean creatures, like the kind of short-haired dog that chases others in a park. Their lithe muscularity, and if they aren't fixed, their dangling balls, can't help but make people see them as sexual creatures, panting grins, playfully biting the necks of other dogs.

I'd seen owners watching their dogs play like that, from afar, standing by the side, leashes ready while they talked of their dogs with other owners.

People would watch us like that, Griffin and I, in bars, in restaurants, anywhere. It was as if they were imagining us together, and not envying one or the other, but the union, the space between us.

21

October. I hadn't gotten a haircut in months. I hadn't shaved in over a week. I looked awful. Terrific.

I planned to not cut my hair for a year, hoping to take on that Brat Pitt *Kalifornia* look, or some sort of fashion pale sultry *Details* model-long-hair-always-falling-in-my-face ideal.

It felt pretty weird, but I was doing it deliberately to repel men, to see who would look at me if I didn't have a terrific short crop, to see who would see beyond the trend, who would care enough, who was attracted to my look. I didn't want men coming into my bed and failing to erase him.

I'd given up on those stupid earrings. Two holes and not a one worth plugging. You could say the same about a few other holes. But those earrings. I kept losing them. They kept falling out, kept reminding me of Griffin. I wanted to become sexually invisible, untouchable, unruly, unattractive, truly sense that, know my problems.

People I knew said things about me, as if a comment here or there might put it back together, their image of me, so they wouldn't feel uncomfortable, like looking at a painting that is off-center. One cannot resist the urge to nudge it just so.

And yet I looked at longhaired boys differently. When you buy a Volkswagen, all you see on the highway are other Volkswagens. The idea of a man's hair falling on my face did not particularly attract me. The longhaired men I'd been with, so few, did not compel me. Things changed.

I had lunch with Harlan since he was back in town.

"It will not look good, like those models," Harlan said, running his hand disdainfully through my strands.

"I have to get some hair thing at a salon," I defended. "Thickener."

But he reminded me that I had no low hairline, no thick locks like shanks of hair that make men want to run their fingers through it. It's light and curls in the wrong places and is feathery and wispy and messy. If I could only get beyond the stage of wanting it to be long, of accepting this mid-state of mess.

I missed rubbing the scalps of men with crew cuts, cherished the moments I rubbed Harlan's head and his short skull. How I loved talking British gibberish with him, popping into cockney or French Canadian at a moment. Did any of his muscle hunk fucks do that, I wondered? Did any of them know anything about his music? Did he talk about these things with them? I didn't think so. What did they have that I didn't, besides gorgeous bodies? His long-term loves were men like me, thin, attractive dark-haired men, and weasels, and capable of intensity and betrayal.

I could offer all that to him, but devotion, too. I wanted so much to just grab him and force a kiss out of him, he wouldn't even kiss me on the lips anymore, knew my desire, feared infection, another OI, turned his head for a brotherly hug, afraid of me, my potential for obsession and love. It was all right in my face, right there, which was why I didn't call him after our lunch, or go out or call him for weeks.

I had decided to take some swimming classes at City College, but that was months ago that I registered, when the world was full of hope.

It was cold and dark on nights, and so rainy I didn't take the bike, because it was also having problems, crank shaft or something, and I was too exhausted to get it fixed, so I regularly caught the N-Judas, and solemnly waited under the bus stop.

Of course, to top it all off, we get our first deluge of a rainy season. I wore my CPO every day, just to fend off the chills and dampness, warmed by the little memories of our wild Uniform Night together.

I liked was going to the pool, and even that was so short-lived, the thrill of swimming and seeing other guys, not at all like the gyms at school, so vacant, but on campus there are so many cute young men, none of them looking back, so absent, the rush of desire, the tension, the desperation, not even any cruising. It was like the fog out here, cool, breezy ephemeral, intangible, escaping, always escaping.

With goggles on, you can swim low as a cute guy crosses the pool, check his body, see him see you in those creature eyes.

I did this often, and a few times ended up chatting with a guy while lathering up in the twenty-head shower, getting sort of hard, smirking, trading numbers, or just, "See ya," if he seemed too remote, which was most of the time. Maybe it was me.

There was a bathroom incident, though.

Cruising was a fumbling, stumbling skill, and I spent too much time gazing at loping straight boys, or double- and triple-glancing gay boys without the skills of introduction or seduction.

I'd heard about the library, and only jacked off in the tiny restrooms in "the stacks," but never bagged a boy among the tomes of literature.

But I'd heard about a certain restroom in the basement. I had no idea where I got that dish; perhaps just innate gaydar. I had to whack off somewhere, and besides, I wanted to blow off class. Boy, did I blow off class.

I sat a while, well, two seconds, before I noticed the air. Because of the two doors, several feet apart, there was a quiet serenity to the white-tiled rest room. Birds chirped from behind the shrubs that covered the basement window.

Footsteps, the door, then a guy sat down in the stall to my left. A bit of odd toe-tapping led my eye to the white high-tops, shucked whiter socks, a rumple of red sweat pants, powder-furry blond legs, and over the floor, the shadow of movement, back and forth, back and forth.

First, the knees entered under the stall. The hair, pale white and all over, tugged my tongue down. I collapsed beside the toilet and licked.

Then, sproinging out of the middle, his bone hard erection, red and clean. I slurped, banging my nose against the low metal rim of the stall wall, the first cock since Griffin.

Somehow, my finger got into my mouth, and trailed up between his legs. I found his bunghole under more fur. It kissed the tip of my finger, then sucked it in a bit, clamping down. His hand stopped me.

I shoved my pants down and shoved my knees between his. We straddled each other like two forks of leg, the wall blocking our upper torsos.

A warm wet gooey tickle oozed over the head of my cock, then slooped downward, swallowing the whole rod. A hand cupped my balls. I smeared my face over the graffiti-coated walls, then noticed dried trails of spew.

We traded back and forth for about half an hour, me sucking his red erect cock, slathering my drool over it, letting it drip down onto the cold marble floor, until a guy came in, pissed, washed and left.

We had frozen back up to sitting, our rigid cocks drying from the coat of spit, aching.

That made us nervous. Classes were ending. There'd be a herd of guys aching to piss and shit in a few minutes. The moment was now.

We returned back to our kneeling positions. He fisted his dick while I frantically choked my own, then I knelt down again to suck him some more. A spew of sperm spat out, hitting my face, landing in creamy globs on the floor, I raced to slurp up the bits from my fingers, and almost knelt down to lick the floor, when his hand reached out and grabbed my cock. I felt his tongue and lips again and shot into him. He wouldn't stop licking until I'd long stopped gushing.

We retreated to our seats just as another guy came in. We waited for his exit, then he got out. I stood, and watched him wash his hands and face. Scared to follow, he glanced back once, but then left.

I couldn't follow him right out. My cock wouldn't go down. By the time I raced up to the steps and outside, he was gone.

I searched the campus for the remaining weeks, but the red sweats and that face never appeared again, disappeared among the departing flock of Christmas break.

Having that surprise sex unleashed my anger at the world, and at myself, for losing Griffin. I had a horrible argument with my boss about going back to New York for a trip. Like it's a crime to go out of town for Christmas. Fuck the magazine. It'll keep.

I'd already ordered tickets to *Angels in America,* which I hope to see with an old boyfriend, who was doing well, then plane tickets.

But the real reason was just to get back to my apartment (Subletter pal upstate with his family), sift through my stuff, and especially to see once again that one porno magazine with the Puerto Rican hunk I saw at the Gaiety, and maybe to go there, and see boys dance around and show their dicks.

So much like The Nob Hill back in San Francisco, but different, special, historic, where the men just walk around in the audience from one customer to another, more a meat show for hookers.

Not that the Gaiety isn't that, but the format allows for more admiring of them, their bodies, the way they arrive on-stage with hardons, like art, like a real dance, to be admired for their cocks, precious, worth watching, worth the admission.

So sordid, my reasons for returning to New York, it seemed a lost mission, a desperate thing. I hoped to get lost, to spend time with Jewish friends, Nat and Jason and David, ignoring this holiday on what would be my first time in New York for Christmas.

All those years, those years living there, and I never stayed in the city. I lied to my parents that I'd only have time on Christmas day. As a tourist, I would be there, and I was gonna prepare for the loneliness, the possibility of sleeping in a lonely hotel if the old boyfriend wouldn't take me in, or anywhere, or even debasing myself into looking for a cheap cock suck night with some equally lonely guy on Christmas. How desperate could I get? How low can we go?

I intended to find out.

"One desires a naked world of love to replace the one of lonely dailiness, a world which has a heat of emotion and genital heat, and such warm, shocked brightness spreading through it that it might as well be Hell."

   – Harold Brodky,
   Profane Friendship

22

**Forgetting Griffin
a hejira**

159. (The numbers continue after my earlier adventures from high school up to recently; for another book.)

Back in a New York groove.

After some sleep, ate stuff, watched B-ball at my straight friend Jeff's while smoking pot. We're old friends, back to '80s, when we went to college together. He's got a great record collection.

It's nice to have men friends who you don't get you tangled up in the sex thing. I know, you're thinking I'm a cock hungry fool and how could I befriend a het? But the thing about these men is that they can't, or won't take that other step into knowing a guy.

Their cocks may taste fine as wine on a summery hill, but if they don't even wanna chat, well, you've got yourself some short-term disappointment.

It was nice to visit, but more comfortable to stay with the old boyfriend, a term I use endearingly. We'd been through so much together, heartaches and passion, that if and when we resumed any sexual fun, it was more like a class reunion, slightly strange, but mostly comfortable.

Home by eleven thirty, remembered M.'s sex party at the Bijou, absolutely made up for all the badness of Saturnalia. All the boys were there. Denton P., J.W.P., other P., R.G., M., J.G., et all. And it seemed a double dose of short thick beautiful men was in order.

After fondling the distant bearded redhead's chest, watched the JO trio that got the backroom's attention. But they were doing the "don't touch me" silliness, and I wasn't hard yet. A semi-attractive thin creature approached from behind, undid me, we chest-humped, I felt his furry light bit of pecs. Bad breath. People watching.

Then, the shortest, beautifullest, goateed black-haired little guy approached. One grip of the thick hard dick assured it. I plopped my cock out of some other creature's mouth. Dismissed, thank you.

Tumbled together with the little muscle wonder and loved letting him take control. Sucked the tastiest, freshest slab o' dick. Didn't taste of previous slobbing, but you never know.

I let him be a mean thing, shoving my mouth back and forth. Crawled my hands up to rounded pecs, licked up to his belly button and nibbled his nipple. We grazed noses, rubbed cheeks, licked his neck, nibbled his ear, ran my fingers through the short cut. Hooray for my short cut, which has given me more looks on the street than a wagging ass. Hooray for Astor Place instant cuts. Ten bucks wisely invested.

Obeying the little man's shoving my head back down to the cock of life, I sucked more as he shoved the back of my head against the cheap paneled wall, but then, wisely stood and whispered in his ear, "Zip up and we'll get a booth." He followed and I saw Denton P., my good luck charm, it seems. We asked a lonely man to please let us use the last open room for a few minutes.

A few minutes indeed.

Shirts and coat off, pants around our ankles, I clamped down on that cock for all it was worth.

He was up for it, being a mean boy, teasing, whapping it against my face, slamming it down to my tonsils, jacking while I kissed its ruby end, lipstick gloss of a piss head. I wanted more, and tried hard to keep my hands on a body part at every moment; thick thighs, furry butt tightly clenched, pecs, arms, tool, thick neck.

Of course he wouldn't kiss, the little beast, wouldn't kneel for me. Who cares, I can get that from any old queer, this little man needed to be big, high, exalted.

I turned him around and fished my tongue into a furry ass of sweet, surprisingly unsalty sweat. Licked the frenum, sucked the balls into my mouth. He spread his legs and got my head down on the bench, while I jacked myself to near spitting quite a few times. My cock mashed against his calf. He jacked his dick and winced. Then came the flood.

I opened my mouth, catching the squirt right on my lips, then my nose, then my brow. Damn, I wanted to watch it, taste it, feel it, but the spew got in my eye, so I had to squint.

Glistening in the red light, inches from my eyes, I looked up at him and shot up onto his leg. Wanted to stay there a while, but we didn't, of course. I wiped my forearm over my face.

"Sorry."

"No problem." I wanted to lick it up. At least I didn't swallow the bolts of jizz, as much as I was damn sure about this guy's HIV status, but then, who knows?

Later, dishing with J.W. in the loo after hot water soapy washing my hands and face, I scanned the GMHC safer sex chart. Yup. Ten demerits. The little stud was still wandering around half an hour later as I chatted at the bar with M.W. K.D. and J.H. Ahh, cookies and soda. Satiated, I still enjoyed watching *Spokes* on the monitor, especially the mustached guys.

Oh, by the way, after the sex with the little guy, retrieving our strewn clothes in that tight booth of bliss, I'd said, "Duh," pointing to the clothes hooks we hadn't noticed in our frenzy. Oh well, with all that sweatin' going on they needed laundered anyway.

Before going out, I gave him my card, too. But I knew he wouldn't call. I could just see his girlfriend up on 198th Street wondering where he'd been all night.

Or else I'd see him here again, and nowhere else.

The thought made me want to drink down a Rolling Rock and say, "Fuck this."

160. The New York snow gave me a fuzzy energy. I'd called a bunch of guys to meet at Wonder Bar. About three showed up. So pissed off was I that I went right to Tunnel Vision, but saw G. W. and a few other people I really didn't want to see. Enough of that. Went to Bijou 82 and watched porno, almost got it on with a guy, but he chose an older guy with a huge cock.

I peeked over the stall wall barrier to watch a lanky military guy get it from a chunky Latino guy, then strolled about and, behind the screen, started fondling with a chunky blond. We had a nice audience for a while, but decided to "get a room."

He was nice, former fat boy who works out, nice cock and ass, we sucked reciprocally, and he jacked me off I jacked him off and boy did he spew.

He liked me and we talked afterward. He works at one of the comic companies and actually draws Spider-Man! Wish I'd know that when I was sucking his cock. It was almost like watching Spidey shoot spunk! His goo hung from the wall, a glistening web.

We traded cards. Will definitely want to see him again. I went back home, feeling almost guilty, but not quite.

Weeks later, I got a package from the Spidey guy with comic books, and a nice letter.

164. Forget the myth that Wednesday nights are slow for sex. Cluster Fuck certainly wasn't crowded, and that was good, since there were fewer handsome dudes to distract.

Watched some porn, then watched guys jerk their gerkins. Felt up a leather-coated Neapolitan blonde, removed in his way, hard under his jeans but wouldn't let me open the prize. I licked his thick fingers by his crotch instead, while a guy blew another to our left.

Fun areas were not so fun, but being sober and determined to bag the best, I waited, saw a guy I used to know. We didn't greet. Walked in on the Neapolitan watching two daddies get it on. He was still iffy and walked off after I fondled him more, so I fondled the older guys, one smooth and muscley, the other burly bellied, he shot. I tried to get some on my pants. The other didn't come, but I sucked his biceps and they finished, joking about relaxing after a visit from his parents. We laughed loud, scaring the voyeurs.

Saw a tall wide-framed type, made a point to dump the standoffish pretty one and bag the big guy. Wouldn't you know it, he was getting blown on one side and butt-humped on the other in a dark backway.

I watched, jerked, got big boy's attention, he shoved the sucker away, then shoved me down to kneel. I choked while he slammed into me, not ramming, just keeping it there while he smacked and fondled my face, then pulled me up and grabbed my chest, pulled my arms away, forcible, choking my dick till I grunted, then shoving me down again.

I shucked my pants down, grabbed his undies and thick thighs, nestled in on his fuzzy balls and clenched ass. He slammed it into me again, a big yet manageable cock. I had to spit out all the mucal goo he erupted from my mouth, then he stuck it in me again, smacking my face hard many times.

I usually hate that stuff, but I imagined him a tough wide-bodied footballer coming in on me in the locker room while I was sniffin' jocks, him deciding to give me some punishment, let him smack me, slap me while I impaled my skull on his tool.

He let me pull away a moment while another guy sidled up and pulled his pants down, while the tool wagged at my face I slurped on the head like a warm popsicle and came, just gushed thick goo all over his shoes. He didn't even know.

I stood, looking him in the eye, not even seeing the many others who watched. He tried to shove me down again, but I enjoyed pulling away, lowering only down long enough to kiss it one last time. Then pulled away, in control all along. Pulled my pants up in brighter light, washed off and departed. Burp.

The old boyfriend and I decided to go out drinking at The Bar before considering McSex at the nearby hump joint. Saw Curt Fenton, one of many unrequited loves from my early New York days. Tall, thin frame, incredible profile, strong Roman nose, puppy eyes. Hair cut short winter cap style. We caught up, chatting while scoping boys. He seemed simultaneously flirty and removed. Easy to talk about sex, as long as it's not between us. I wondered about bringing it up.

After the second beer, I did. He blushed, feigned disinterest.

Curt's one of those guys who only does guys from out of town, or strangers, or malcontents. Makes sure to engage with those who can't become boyfriend material. I'd resent it if it weren't that I'm in that mode now, too.

But it's more crash recovery, not a way of life. I want to find someone for a long-term thing, maybe, but sometimes it just seems like too much to get involved in.

But then I see Curt's face in half-silhouette, and I think, this is a face worth traveling three thousand miles to see.

165. Back to San Francisco for the final months of my magazine gig. Among the stack of mail was a royalty check from A Different Light for DOGZ, the West Coast edition.

I never published it again.

Back to the Sex Mall.

After a nice party near Coit Tower, yakking it up w/ R.G., R.P. and V. in Caffe Roma, then home, then biking out, thought about going to the gay strip joint, but it was way down there.

Thought about going to Alley Scat or whatever it was called, but didn't know if it would be really sexy fun, so went back to Church of the Homo Organ. Damn cheerful blond chunky door guy, my blessing.

Hit on the cute little (Latino?) guy, crotch groping. He coughed, hadda get a drink, then I bumped into S.S. we chatted, then off to Playland, a bit of round-about, not too many cuties, but caught up with a little hot one. So did many others. He yanked my cock while I licked his nips and neck.

A few mouths were blowing us. The line to get to his cock was longer than some nightclub urinals, so I knelt around back and licked and chewed his tight butt cheeks, nestling my tongue down into his anus and tangy ring of butt muscle. Jerked off to that taste, that winking tang. Stood, shook the come off my hand, shoulda licked it, wiped on his pants, dressed, told the doorman, "Thanks. I came what I got for," then rode Rose home, the smell of that young guy's tangy butt wisping through my whiskers. yum.

As usual, getting hard again just thinking about it, may have to jack off again.

166. Got the urge, despite telling Harlan over the phone that I'd take things into my own hands. I guess I did. I got dressed in my red pants, worried that they'd be too too, thought of shaving my balls, then thought about blood cut transmission, thought of shaving my goatee down to a droopy sidebar western mustache like Rick, or Prick or whatever his name was who totally snubbed me, even though we'd been introduced about five times.

I saw him ambling up the street from Cala on the way to the bank. His arms loped like a monkey as he hiked up Collingwood with some small fry, shopping bags in his hand. That's how to snag a man like that, make him dinner.

Anywhose, with no date, I figured porno and my hands weren't enough. Besides, I could be a little late to work on Thursday.

I dressed and snuck out, worried what sleeping neighbors would think (as if I should care) and stopped by the bank for some cash. Two pairs of leather queers at the machines, no worries about mugging.

The whole of Folsom was slightly alive with desire.

Went right to That Place, even though I'd copied addresses of sex clubs as yet untrod from a local rag, and had a nice flirt with a leather man tying up his motorbike while I U-locked Rose.

Had a beer, had saved some piss, which I hoped to nicely drain in the loo with an audience. As I had thought, it was by far quite a bargain, with more out in the open sex action than any skanky sex club, and the Rolling Rocks only two bucks.

I sidled up to the piss trough, a nice pile of ice there, but the cracked mirror was distracting since two guys were watching me try to piss my willy while another guy was getting his uncut wiener drank from a kneeling piss fan. Should have asked him to empty my bladder.

Anyway, a burly daddy with a cap and bare chest and black leather jacket unbuttoned and out came a long thick cock I immediately prized. I just stood and looked at it, half-grinning, half-dopey, like the late Eric Stryker in that fuck flick before he sits on the hot dad. I watched him just tug it to its full length, and then ambled out, quite obviously having spied my prize for the night.

No need for more shopping, the others though, having fun leaning on the pool table and of course going at it in Das Rhinegold Alley, where the daddy caught up with me and I brushed my knuckle against his crotch. We shopped for a spot, and he led me right past four or five kneeling men all treating on a cock. I liked rubbing their bobbing balding heads. They watched as we ambled down to the brightly lit, then dark end of the alley, the grate behind us and the street sidewalk only inches away.

I knelt quite succinctly, and the tops of my boots attracted a crowd behind us. Daddy's dick was quite a tasty thing, not too funky, but certainly long, and he pulled me up by my collar and let me suck on his nips which were like pencil erasers, only tastier.

Then it was back down and boy was it big, like a small boat. I slurped it and let it gag my throat, but I knew how to breathe through my nose, and then he offered me a popper snort, which in this case felt terrific going in, what with the street breeze only inches away, and on either side of his hips I saw people walking by oblivious, or knowing and not caring.

I slurped and choked and sucked, and he was a bit drunk on some whiskey breath, but we soft-kissed and hugged and then I grabbed it and he mumbled stuff and I let him write his phone number and the name Arthur on the paper and pen I had smartly brought with me, with the list of now unneeded sex clubs on the other side.

He might be fun later, I figured, but may require too much work to get off. I was hard and stiff, and wanted to suck more, but he obliged my rod and knelt to suck, too much teeth at first, but then I fucked his face and showed him the light.

Half a dozen others were behind us, included a drag queen of some fame (out of drag that night), who grinned in appreciative whim, knowing as did I that a fellow as skinny and longhaired as he has a rough time getting popped in a place that prefers the men short and bristly.

I let a handsome Black man fondle my chest while we both got blown by an enthusiastic Latino guy, and Daddy on his knees was working me right.

He leaned his hand over and was, I guess, wriggling his other hand between the tongue of another gent who licked the chunky ass of the other man.

It was a living Tom of Finland, second cast, touring company, and I liked it, wanted it to last, but wanted very much to get off just this way.

Dad began jacking my cock while sucking, and that is magic to my tool, for he pulled away a half second before I spewed, ropey white blobs.

I clutched the cold pipe running along the alleyway, the most wonderful cool feeling, like all the sensations of cheap alley sex only in this comfy environment, like how *West Side Story* is not really in a street, but warm and choreographed violence. Richard Beymer and Russ Tamblyn eating each other's spunk. Shooting contests in an alley. Sperm to Worm.

I tingled and quivered, having grunted a few times, as Daddy gripped my dick, then nestled his face in my groin, then stood, and we hugged, and he said how he wanted to make love to me. Yeah, I thought, but that was pretty nice doing it right here, if you don't mind.

We went out, me wanting to just leave my pants undone to show off my spent-ness, but I buckled up, bought another beer.

A bit later, Dad sidled up to me at the bar, said he went to wash up, and I told him I was negative, "just so you don't have to worry." It didn't seem like he cared, but I did.

I downed my beer. Dad was off to other prospects. I saw other younger tastier ones, but was truly spent in a warm glowing way.

Goodness, this beats those silly sex clubs. The music's better, the sex atmosphere's right out in your face, and they serve beer.

Sure, there's those that have their arguments against that. Take the DSTL, the Dick-Sucking Temperance League. Then there's the SSS, the Society for Safest Sex. They get their noses under every new scene that happens. Drive people to private parties or even their homes.

Sure, they throw a good line about safe sex, and get thousands of dollars to make pretty bus posters advertising it, but what about those who wanna smoke a little herb, or maybe wanna get tied up? Who are they to interfere? We're scared enough as it is. And why are they always pushing condoms on us when there's about a hundred wonderful sex positions two or more guys can do together that don't involve sticking your cock up a guy's butt?

See, I thought some of these San Francisco experiences might lead to some nice fuck buddy relationships. Sometimes that happens.

Other times, you can heat 'em up, drill 'em silly and pump 'em shooting, but come that happy little collision at the Safeway, and they're as faint as the fog.

167. Went to the Nob Hill Theatre to see Ronnie Viera, a total fuck god whom I would commit a felony to fuck. Instead, I merely took the zen risk of riding to the Tenderloin, wondering if I'd find the newly repaired Rose still parked on the street upon leaving.

As I had suspected, he didn't jerk off onstage, but his strip was magic, his dancing, his dangling cock, uncut, juiced up.

He was a huge boy, naturally furry in all the right places, and since they're so restrictive about touching the gonads, he merely let me bury my face in his ass for about three seconds, but that was enough to remember the taste, and the glistening joy of his cock, the sparkle in his eyes as he stood over me, jacking himself slowly to full boingy erection, and me wishing I had a few hundred handy to afford him, if he was a rent boy, too. Need I ask.

Wish I had. He worked the crowd slowly, got to me second, I felt his thighs, torso, belly button tits, golden. I'm practicing how to be a dirty old man.

I fondled the stripper's shoes wrapped around my body like living arm rests. Then he rose up to standing, tugging his boner above me, leaning back to jerk his cock. When Ronnie finished stripping and slowly retreated to his next fan, I came in my shirt, a creamy thick gush.

It took sitting through the next much less talented stripper to recover from my terpsichorean ejaculatory bliss.

I then rode by some nighttime fair in Civic Center, watching stupid carnival rides outside City Hall while wolfing down a Burger King dinner. Trashy day, no?

I should add all the names of the studs that I jacked off at the strip club, but it would almost take up half page. Brandon, Charlton, Jason, etc. I choose not to number them because it was really only a sort of half-sex with some private booth hand-job action downstairs.

But mostly it was what I loved, a glistening rubber-banded cock bouncing in my face as I tucked $5s and $20s into their sneakers, socks or into their boots.

168. Speaking of boots; Folsom Street Fair. I'm writing Thursday before it, and I better have something good to write in here by Monday morning.

I've got something to write, but, well...

After doing the Drummer Boy thing, and the 7th on Sale thing with Denton, and feeling quite melancholy after all that free booze, I didn't call him on Saturday and went out to the Drummer Contest alone. It drew me in, with all its fun. Saw Gary, whom I would like to have some day, and saw others so many strangers, none of them, not a one speaking to me.

Saw Brett from L.A., who looked completely attractive but inappropriate in leather, evasive as usual, but his friend was all over me. We flirted amongst ourselves on the street. I thought for sure I'd met my night's magic, but as I led the black-haired beauty to Rose, he became duly unimpressed and said how the drugs were making him feel unsexual. Yeah, right.

He went dancing. I went to Cluster Fuck, the Discount Cock Emporium, ridiculously busy, and did the wander, waiting for something worth touching.

Surprisingly, there was a most boyish type, one whom I usually don't look at twice, but there was something... French, something, so sad and winsome about him, and lanky, yet a tight striation of muscle, across him. He caught on, and as we stood side by side, I leaned over and touched his chest, crisscrossing his sternum and grazing his breastbone. He led me into a booth where we got down to it, his cock already sprung up from his baggy shorts. He was indolent, yet totally desired by all the others, and I kept having to shove Cocteau-like grasping arms away behind me as my mouth traveled his torso and hips.

I got down to it and resolved to impale my mouth on his cock, and allowed a beautiful yet pushy Asian man to kiss him. I watched from below, trying to control a fit of jealousy, he trying to get the cock. I lightly grazed the Asian, who wanted it all, but wouldn't give in, and soon, soon, the young boy exploded into my mouth. I shot up against his thigh.

I swallowed another man's sperm for the first time in years.

That made me forget about Griffin for a while.

We nodded silently as we left. I scruffed the back of his neck, and the little Asian led him out like Gretel leading Hansel from the witch's oven.

Although I didn't have sex at the Folsom Street Fair, I'll note that I bumped into Bill S. and his pup, also Kevin C. again, in his black jacket, and went and had a strange, good, if not unfocused time with Ted and Artie, both New York friends now in medical school at UCSF.

Artie was thick and mixed Italian-Greek, a buffet of muscles and prominent features, a nose as thick as his cock, I'd heard. Ted was lanky and witty, a cougar on the prowl. Yes, we were high.

Artie kept putting his hand on my back, leading me through crowds. He made me feel good, wanted, maybe. I did so many stupid things in front of him, saying so many gushing compliments that he probably never even sees me at night when he beats off. If he does, the little pack of muscle and frustration and facts probably gets off more on, who knows, anything but me.

Ted preened coolly in his gear, while I posed as Mr. Leather Dude Thing, to the amusement of Denton and Vic, who we finally found amid the endless parade of beauties and half-beauties and odd characters in straps and chaps for the day, indifferent or too tweaked to make eye contact.

Artie and I got stoned. I walked by a handsome man pissing behind a car, leaned over and licked his piss stream, much to the disgust of all present. Oh well.

We sat and talked on sunny steps, and watched the parade of men go into the tent. We danced in the tent a few minutes, and then I knew I liked Artie a lot.

"You like that stuff?" he asked, curious.

"What, piss?"

"Yeah. Kinky stuff."

"With the right guy."

"But he was a total stranger."

"But he was the right sort of guy."

"You're strange."

"Too strange for you, huh?"

"Yeah."

"Sorry about that."

Relaxing at home while Ted napped, stripping off our leather gear like melted armor, I enjoyed giving Artie a foot massage, loved having him almost naked on my bed, but didn't enjoy having to tell him that he could do the same for me, which he did, but without a hint of desire. He could rant about biopsies, infarctions and all kinds of stuff. He was gloriously self-absorbed, wonderfully insecure, and utterly chunky, a total meal, with leftovers for the next morning.

But the best, the best thing was when I popped into loose shorts and returned to the living room to see Artie, who wore nearly the same shorts. We were like Ritchie Cunningham and his bud and right then "Rock Around the Clock" came on the radio, and we danced a Lindy in my living room, arm in arm, whirling, buds, innocent.

That was the best part of the day and better than sex.

That was what I missed, not cocks, not asses, not mouths, but joy between men.

169. After Carefree (a.k.a. Brainfree), Ted let me take his and Artie's car, so I went to The Cock Factory and the very first guy I glanced at was absolutely hot and took me in a booth, and even though I was still damp from dancing, he was warm and furry and muscular, and we kissed and played and sucked, and nibbled, and he wanted me to piss on him, but too bad, I was completely dehydrated from dancing. I even went and drank some water, but that didn't help.

So we necked and licked and sucked, awkwardly standing, our pants around our ankles, rimming butt, leaning on the bench. Over us, the glow-in-the-dark spacescape on the upper walls of the sex space glowed above the dark glow of sex in the booths. The B52s song, "Revolution Earth," came on the sound system.

"And we know that we're alive, if we weren't sure before."

I thought of Griffin and his rejection of me one night while that song played. I had to let him go, but this man whose name I never learned, this man wanted me with all the force two bodies can find in a wooden hole-filled booth. Letting his cock flop from my mouth, wet and stiff, I knew we were alive.

I lapped his cock as it lay hard against his thigh. His cock ring helped him stay hard. No mind, we came. He gushed while standing, I while sitting and licking. Good, but he left the booth so soon, and I didn't get to give him my number. Off in search of the magic elixir, no doubt.

170. Well, dreams do cum true. Planned an evening and got exactly what I wanted. Didn't have a hot date or tickets to the opera, but then again, who wants that stuff when all you really want is some artistic stimulation, some beer and flirting and hot direct action?

Went to a lesbian lit reading instead.

No, seriously, they blew me away with their words, and the partner of one of the authors I knew came by, sitting next to me with their baby. Ah, the joys of turkey basters. Mom #2 still calls me Tim, instead of Tom, my real name, but I guess all fags look alike.

Rode on down to the Eagle, where Mike S. introduced me to Eric and Mike (porn boy), two hunks from the gym.

Reasons to chit chat now, maybe, if they recognize me. SFers are a little spacey on the memory factor.

Hugged Lenny, kissed Andy, who won Mr. Safe Sex. Hope to romance him some day, but now that he's big cheese again it may not be easy.

Settled myself in to the long trek to The Cock Factory, where, something told me a good time would be had. This time I wouldn't be at all dehydrated from dancing like last time. The Eagle beer bust was perfect fuel, and my bladder was tingling for release.

Checked my coat, sauntered in, walked around and headed right into the wet room, knowing full well I'd be walking out with soaked jeans. Pulled my t-shirt off, put my True Valu cap back on, and shucked my jeans down and sidled up to the trough.

Nobody was into it, it seemed, but I had to piss. I closed my eyes to relax, and when I opened them, damned if there weren't a dozen guys around the trough and two guys in it. I love how I can serve as such quick inspiration.

Anyway, a total piss fest ensued. What I had fantasized about for so long became a dream come true.

A guy sucked. I pissed all over him, another pissed near me. I yanked a thick dick, then bent over to suck another, and another hand yanked my pud.

Then a warm trickle on my bare jock strap butt fell over me. Another guy across the way spurted jumpy droplets. I grabbed hold of the trough and straddled it, exposing my ass, which got played with major. Then I grabbed a guy's neck and sucked and bit it. A beautiful chunky guy in a black t-shirt pissed all over himself and I licked his wet t-shirt, and yanked his pud as he came. More piss flying in all directions.

I tasted some, all crystal clear, not bitter at all. Musta been beer piss. The guy in the black t-shirt oinked and we all laughed.

Sucked a guy's big fat honker good, and he told me to kneel, I shucked my pants down and knelt, then he pissed on me. I licked his cock as it spurted a stream, then a big chunky leather man forced me down and I licked leather like no tomorrow.

I got a hit of amyl, got majorly felt up and appreciated, loved, as it were, and licked his little peter and shucked my pants down again and got on all fours and licked his boots while he smacked my ass, not nearly hard enough or long enough, but enough to get me going. I slurped his dick while he pissed in my mouth.

I let it build up in my mouth, let it dribble over my chin, and yanked my cock, and then leaned back and let hands take over, as I came and came and let his piss pour out of my lips and down my chest. I felt so fucking full and wet and good and bad.

The crowd pulled away, and I shucked my soaked pants up. I put my cap on, and rearranged my damp shirt behind my butt, tucked my cock in.

Went and sat down in the lounge to relax and take it all in, then checked out, rode Rose, proudly/embarrassedly waiting at the light on the street outside the Endup in my piss wet soaked jeans in the streetlight. Zoomed home, shivering from the coat of wet men juice.

Came home, showered, washed my shirt and jock and jeans in the shower, washed with my pilfered bacterial soap (which I stole from a college football locker room) and made sausages and eggs and toast and thought about men I'd been with, men I'd peed with, how some seemed to hint about wanting it, but never came out and said or did anything about it.

Like the time I lay in the tub with Griffin the First, back in New York, a million years ago.

Wrapped around each other's legs, he'd let go with a high arcing stream that trickled down into the tub water. I'd moved to lap it up, but he'd just shoved me back. I leaned back all right, and started lapping up the tub water, just to spite him, just to get it.

The chasm between men who will and men who can't widens. I'll be back to the trough, I guess, if I need a refill.

171. The night of the Harvey Milk memorial march, I went to the gym, then rushed out at 7:30, worried I'd missed it, when of course my timing was dead on, and as I approached Market and Laguna, the group, smaller than I expected, was marching. I'd brought a little votive, not one of the big Catholic candles, because I figured, hey, Harvey's watching, maybe I might meet a guy.

Sure enough I did. Saw a silent one from the gym, but he was his usual brooding neurotic self, and Mike S. was fun, and Mike B. was his warped DPN self, and later I saw Donnie, but it was after I'd got my arms around Jed.

We were walking shoulder to shoulder, my hand in his butt pocket of his jeans, and when we got to City Hall, then is when he got it, saying, "I didn't know you wanted to play," and I was like, duh, and he said, "Well, you have to say it." I guess one has to be blunt in this town. It sometimes works.

Anyway, we ended up giggling in the back, barely hearing what the speakers were saying, and then we kissed, I mean really kissed, and the candles flickering, and a TV camera was in the background interviewing a family, and we were remembering Harvey on the anniversary in a city that tries to, but never forgets.

We walked along afterward, and Jed said he had to piss, and fortunately we didn't go in some place respectable, but found an alley off Van Ness, and he peed and I did my best not to watch, but then he got it and kissed me again, and scrunched down on his knees between two garbage dumpsters. I let him suck me even though the dumpster smell reminded me of awful jobs in restaurants, rotting food, decay, but his teeth were getting to me, he was eating my cock, and a car zoomed by.

"Damn," I said. "Let's get someplace respectable."

Fortunately, we'd been walking toward my place, even though he'd been talking about his boyfriend all this time, I didn't care.

We got home, got naked and started in kissing and sucking, and Jed went to town, and I licked his back and his butt cheeks and he rimmed me good. His goatee tickled, and I liked it, then he clamped down on the cock, and I did him, but it tasted gamey, and it wasn't huge, but I liked his body and I liked him, and then we're 69ing, me not really sucking his cock, since I knew he was positive. He told me.

He jabbed a finger up my butt, then expertly finger-fucking my ass and jacked my cock, and I shot, boy I shot while sucking his balls. Then he straddled me and played with my dick while I sucked his balls, both in my mouth, and I felt his come splat on my belly, and it was good.

Jed lay down and we talked, er, he talked and I listened, a tale of boyfriends dead and girlfriends dead and family dead, and I saw his pale bubble butt and would have liked to fuck him, but he said, "Gotta be going," so we walked on out and I had to go to the bank anyway, so we got to the Castro and saw Bobbie Bubble, who said, "How's his ass?"

The funny bitch. We were practically oozing good sexy feelings and Jed greeted all kinds and introduced me and we had pizza at Marcello's and it was great, amazing stuff, and then we walked back and I walked him home to his house where he was gonna move out of the next day. I mentioned wanting to be his dog, and wanting to do some SM stuff, and it was nice, but not for real, since he had a boyfriend.

A day later, Saturday I think, I rode Rose all the way up to Twin Peaks and lay on some shrub flat part and jacked off in the sun. I rode back down, passed by Harlan's, but he wasn't home.

172. After a pot-filled dinner party, I walked home, still the remainder of my toasted condition stirring my libido, and I looked for any listing of Mike's Cluster Fuck, but none. Was it closed? I chanced it and remembered the big jock who slam mouth-fucked me, hoping to find him or someone like him, knowing I wouldn't and I'd be lucky to find anyone I could get hard with, wham, I go in and there's a cut shave head lowering himself to worship me. Life is good sometimes.

His head felt just like K.J.'s, an amour from Nuevo Yorke, and I rubbed it and leaned over and licked it.

Some other guys tried to horn in on the action, but I had my man, especially when he stood and let me suck him, and his cock was big and stiff, but with fleshy almost uncut resilient silky skin sliding back and forth as I sucked.

He got back on his knees again, and another guy was crowding to get my dick. I pulled my skinboy over against a wall, and then he stood and we kissed deep. His tongue was a knob of darting wetness. I grabbed him and licked his ears and he jacked me and some guy was on his knees sucking but I shoved him away. He was some Eurotrash tourist who whispered dirty talk, "I vant you to fuck me, I want to eat your come." *C'est dommage.* I shoved him away, but he hovered and fondled my ass.

I knelt again, then got pulled up, and cute baldy skinboy jacked nonstop and before I knew it he got my hand and leg wet with his spurts, and he was purring, and I took him aside, and didn't let the guy suck me since my dick had skinboy's come on it, and his come was on my hand and I wanted to sneak a lick of it, but I pulled away from the suck queen and kissed my guy and said, "Can you jack me off?"

He clutched it joyfully, tuggin' away and the good feeling was major, and he got on his knees again and this other guy started getting down, but the Eurotrash was on me, and I said, "Arrete."

Skinboy stood and let me shoot copiously on the wall, and we kissed and I licked his neck and it was good, and I saw his face. He had sharp eyebrows, but with the shaved head looked like a lot of guys. I wanted to see him again, but we'd come and the Eurotrash was all over us again, and we pulled up and pulled apart and he said, "Did you come?" "Oh yeah," I said. "Look." Pointed to my Jackson Pollock on the wall.

"Oh yeah."

Riding back, as the rain began to fall harder, I realized that, caught in between my teeth was one of his pubic hairs.

174. When porn star and occasional fuck buddy Vinny Jackson died, he left me his chaps. I'd been scared to even try them on, but one night, the books and tapes weren't enough, so I decided to play dress up.

Tried jacking off with the chaps on, but really wanted to go out, since I missed the Solstice Party, so I got on my bike, chaps creaking as I straddled it, and then went on to the Cock Factory. Leather Night.

Had an incredibly frustrating time trying to get my chaps off, then stripped off my pants and put the chaps back on, so I could let my tight little ass and half-hard cock hang out. Always wanted to do that. But I kept getting leg hairs caught in the zipper, getting some strange glances while working it in that dark dressing area.

Made a complete fool of myself, or got a good long warm-up going, which ever. After a few minutes of frustration, finally got dressed in boots, chaps, collar and cock strap on my wrist.

Wandered around a bit, then went in the piss room, where I immediately found a master for the evening, who only approached when I correctly dropped my head and put my arms behind my back, assuming the position. He took me against a wall and smacked me around good, pissed on my back, made me piss in a cup and drink it, my own, gulp it down. Quite good.

Got me on my knees, after smacking my butt a lot, and my shoulders, and had me suck his cock, which had a Prince Albert pierce. I tasted the metal before I even realized it. The damn silver kept gagging me, though. It was like being attached to a human can opener.

He smacked me around more, then tried to get me to suck some other guy's cock, which was not the idea. I was in control, something I grew to love, looking up into his silhouette, the red light behind his head sort of blinding me to seeing his evil stare, but I calmed him down, while I was truly bored with tuning his nipples.

What are you tuning?

The taste of your tongue. The taste of your cock.

We went out to relax after he proposed doing this some more some other time. I was affectionate in his lap while we sipped sodas. Then he took me to the barber chair and I stood atop him, jacked off on his tit and licked it off.

More action followed, and while I was having fun just watching, I got into a lanky Latino's big thick uncut meat (175), then let a nerdy white guy knelt and blew me (176), although he was not getting me going again.

Fondled a smooth Black man (177), while my master of the moment, was now on his knees sucking my cock, then all three cocks. The Latino then showed off by sucking his own cock, just bending over and doing it. Then I sucked it (178). I was over it, until a bit of poppers, then one man's tongue got hot and twisted itself into my mouth while the Latino sucked me and a handsome nerd (179.5) I swear, black-rimmed glasses, dress shirt, the whole thing) rimmed me. When the nerd stood, I turned around and kissed his cheek, saying thank you.

I had to relax, and the whole scene continued a bit while I sat in the chair, then everybody left and I thought they were all bored with me, until a big burly giant of a man named Ray (179) stood between my legs, jacked me, and hugged me and kissed slow, then humped me slowly, he was so big, a wall of muscle, and a Herculean face, a big Roman nose. We were kissing and I wrapped my legs around him and humped his belly and came so warm and slow after all that SM stuff, it was tingly good. We kissed a lot and chatted, and he started with the boyfriend stuff, and I gradually became really sad because I knew I could do just that with him, but I didn't rate.

He said, "What gym do you go to?"

"Tits R' Us."

"I go to Titans."

"Ah, the big boys."

"You'll be there soon."

Presumptuous of him. Then, while chatting, came upon Ted, who I introduced, and talked with, all the while fondling Ray's huge fingers. We kissed more and that damn sweet song "Revolution Earth" came on again, and sensing my deep dream to sway with Harlan at the B-52s concert, turned me around and danced with me while kissing. Talk about swoon. Wish I'd got his license plate number.

Going home, but first watched by the master for the night while I changed. Odd, I slowly lost all interest in all of them. It's not in the arena. All I thought of was calling some old friend, outside the arena, outside, where warmth and firelight and dinners didn't seem like an afterthought, and sex wasn't just a goal, but something to look forward to for a long time, not a few minutes.

I hope I didn't get any germs or viruses. I got a few welts and scrapes from the zipper on the chaps, and of course from the master. Dreams do come true when, as the clothes-check guy said, "We are slaves to fashion."

180: After going to see *8 1/2* at the Castro Theatre, then dining out with N. and J., T. (now dead), and S., who spoke Italian brilliantly, we had a drink at Rhino Walk, and the group dwindled down, then they went off homeward, and I (must have been those damn socks I wore, the ones I stole from that football locker room) just casually walked into Head games as if I'd been there every night of my life.

Had one beer, and after surveying the scene, oh my, I was so indolent. I couldn't have cared less who was there. I watched the big guy from Thursday night, the big stud swaying, only now he was inches from me and shirtless and doing nasty things with two guys, kissing, jacking off in a corner or whatever. That was amusing, and two head-shaven punks who kept smooching and bumping into my back, and then him.

He wore one of those silly Nazi-like caps, but he seemed nice, and especially nasty. His big brown eyes helped, plus he was tall and, well, a daddy, obviously.

I glanced at the Tom of Finland drawings on the TV while I sat, legs apart on the pool table across from him. We made flirty eyes for a while until he simply nodded for me to come over.

Chit chat, forgettable blah, then another beer and some fondling, where he clutched my ass while I stood, then I clutched his big hard bulge behind me while I stood in front of him, sitting on the bottle crates. The lanky shirtless barback shuffled through, and men continued to flirt.

We got out of there and walked to his place, over on Sanchez. He had grabbed me while walking, a big carnivorous kiss, and also shoved his hand down my pants, fingering my ass as we walked. Oh yes, he was going to do just what I wanted.

He told me to strip the moment we got inside his lovely top floor apartment. He shoved his cock in my mouth, big and stiff and clean, no nasty taste, and then took me in the bedroom and did the chain collar and handcuffs. This was going to be intense. He had me kneel and made me suck, I almost vomited, my gag reflex off-game.

He held a cig for me to suck, a gulp of beer, a popper here and there "No thanks, sir," and also smacked my butt while I bent over and licked his combat boots.

He really worked me over, and had a lovely leather bedspread and played soft pumping disco fag music. He bent me over and worked my ass with his fingers, then forced his cock in and out for a long while.

He put a double chain of nipple clamps on, which hurt like needles, but I knew they would help grow nips, even though I don't care about that stuff. He lay back and had me work him, kept up a good line of repetitive dirty talk that kept me inspired and grunting "Yes sir, fuck me, sir," just about every minute or so.

He fucked me from behind, from on top, rolled me over and I threw my legs back into my handcuffed wrists. He slammed in and out and it hurt, but I wanted it, because sometimes, sometimes, he would slow down and tickle me with just a few inches, which of course I like so much better.

After a good long bout of this butt slamming, yes, he wore a condom, and stayed wonderfully hard, he let me lay back with him, and he jacked off while I lay beside him, suckling on his hairy teats and helping jack him off.

He sprayed all over me, didn't even notice that I hadn't cum, and tossed the rag on my chest, which I said I didn't need yet. I wanted his come splashes to grow cool on my chest as I jerked off and sprayed. Then I needed the rag.

We lay down to sleep like spoons, then he rolled over and I was free to sleep near him, but my dreams were odd, a mirrorlike reflection of what we did, that woozy not quite asleep sleep.

We woke up around 9:30 and I went to work on his cock, wiping away my morning breath on his dick. Still handcuffed, it wasn't easy, but I managed. He liked choking me, but I liked pulling the extra skin up and slathering the head around my face and lips, just slurping on the head.

He had me sit on his dick, and I liked that the best, because my guts were comfortable, I suppose, but sitting on a cock just feels the most comfortable, but then he rolled me over and lay on top of me, and humped me.

I liked that, and thought of John C., how he had cruelly slammed into me those times, leaving me begging for more.

But then he pulled me back and did more doggy, but I had enough and was near tears, my face mashed in the sheets, worried because I didn't think he had a condom on. I had to check, reaching for his cock.

He rolled me over on my back and with my legs not too far up in the air, it felt good and comfortable, because he wasn't slamming, just nice mid-length fucking, and I got so close, so tickled that I was gonna cum without touching it, but at the last moment I had to rub up against his belly to shoot, and I did, ropey splats up against him, but he kept on going, selfish to the last, and I had to beg him to stop, even though I could have let him go on.

I just didn't like that he was just using my butt now, not being a sympathetic daddy, not being caring, and besides the dirty talk didn't really work in the morning. It wasn't that the cap was off (he'd kept it on all through last night), and showed his very bald head, which I liked actually, but that he probably had already forgotten my name and assumed I wanted to just stay there forever like that, getting fucked.

I managed to get rolled over on my side and take a break, but he pulled up against me and fake-fucked my butt sideways, then shoved it in and kept on going. I'd had enough and pulled away, loving the last withdrawal like a clean and final shit, knowing that was it, the last of his fucking for now.

He settled back to the laying back position, and I jacked him and watched him jack his greasy stiff pole, then he said "Pull my balls," which he had been doing last night with the help of a heavy ball on a chain wrapped around his scrotum, and I pulled and it was like a stopper, he shot, just as good a load as last night, and as I humped his thigh I got closer, then jacked off again, the third time.

I fell back to sleep. He did for a bit and then got up to answer a call and make coffee and take a really long shower. I would have joined him but I didn't want to get the jewelry wet.

He finally uncuffed me and took the collar off, but not before handcuffing me to the door knob for a bit, joking about keeping me here.

As if.

I smiled, amused by the possibility, but I think he knew I was done with him. Maybe he didn't.

He undid me and I took a shower, cleaned up, refreshed.

We sat in his living room admiring the view through the pouring rain, Corona Heights right out there. I showed him my good luck pilfered socks (see my story in *Rahm,* "Locker Room Midnight") while I finished dressing, and we sipped tepid coffee and had a cig while he occasionally looked at his watch, impatient to get me out and get going. He seemed a bit off, like he might be just a bit cracked, and I was glad to soon be away.

"It was very intense," I said. I told him how I wouldn't need that for a long time. He may have been offended, but I didn't care anymore. I wouldn't need this for a while, wouldn't want to feel like a piece of meat and at the same time so exalted, so devotedly fucked, so overbaked.

Home, I ate and slept and got a call from Lee about going to a Hawaiian dance concert. The theater was way out in the Avenues, but even through the driving rain, each of us wrapped in rain gear, risking our lives on the flooded road as much as I had last night with a strange man's cock sliding up my ass, I felt vibrantly alive.

The concert was so beautiful, soft movements, then powerful erotic dancing with men in grass skirts, hips thrusting, the head of the company a huge muscular Hawaiian with the most captivating eyes. It was so incredibly touching, feeling slightly like a boy again, wishing to have this kind of magic between being sexually attracted to a man like the leather daddy and liking Lee for a friend.

Finding, wishing to find a man who is a balance of the two, and of course it may have been Griffin, but I can't find him to go back to him. It's burned, gone, ruined. At least it was amazingly fun to get so thoroughly fucked just pretending I was 19 again, and pouty and young and willing.

A day later, my hands still had the circulation cut off in a few places in my fingers. My nipples were sore and marked.

I dropped Lee off and went home, peeling off the layers of rain gear, the night awash in the downpour. A coat of sweat and warm dampness clung to my body. I stood among a pile of yellow skin, coats, shirts, pants, checking my naked frame for marks, bruises, cuts. I started crying for no reason.

181: Sometimes it costs to have a new thrill, like bungee-jumping.

Sometimes you get your money's worth.

I considered going to the Bobbin' Knob Cinema to see hot puppy Ricky Sere dance the dance, and see that locker room secret video. The video was fun, guy after guy wet and naked with dangling dicks and stripping and jock straps, could have watched that a while, but went upstairs to watch Ricky, who beamed as I smiled at him, sitting in the front row.

He sat on my lap, naked and we jacked each other while making chit chat. I complimented his glitter, he let me sniff it. "Nice scent, huh?" I was truly hard.

He went around to the audience, which I always find boring, then, unfortunately didn't even finish by dancing some more or jacking off, didn't even really get hard, except when he sat on my lap. Oh well, now I know both theaters' strippers are a disappointment. They don't dance long enough, don't wag their weenies enough. I longed for the Gaiety.

Went downstairs and watched a campy trippy Fire Island film while chatting with an old gent in some very comfy chairs, like from a seedy library. The film was fun, with betraying lovers and a campy loft lounge queen singing "Just One of Those Things," then trippy artist had a vision of a Colt model jacking off in the woods, his sturdy cock certainly did. It spewed come, but I didn't want to jack off with him, although it would have been nice to have an old gent diddle me.

I wanted to see some new porn to come to, so I went upstairs and watched that cute redhead guy fuck a guy in a locker room (nice finish to that real locker room stuff). Then Danny Somers making out in a pool with mustachioed daddy, getting sucked, getting joyously rimmed, then daddy's threateningly thick cock shoving itself in and out of Danny's mouth, pouty-lipped baby boy, then fucking his buns in a good slow thorough way, getting him to grunt, oh yeah, fuck me daddy, fuck me daddy! which got me going, thinking about J. the leather guy from the other night, and calling him up and going "I need it bad."

Maybe I will, I told myself, but a guy came by and felt my dick, but I was more into myself, and he jumped up and away. Did he think I would follow him when Danny was getting gloriously fucked by his daddy? I jacked and stuck my finger up my ass, rubbing my prostate. As the two shot onscreen, I spewed goo all over myself, on my belly, on my sweatshirt, big gobs. I sucked the cum off my hand and off my sweatshirt and tucked myself in and got up as the credits said THE END.

183. After trying to locate a Joel Dallesandro fuckee hockey jock at some coffee shop that M. talked about, I gave up, but the area was tinged with sex. Went to the gays in the military march, spotted some hot uniformed men. Good speeches. Afterward, M. and Denton and T. and I went to M. and T.'s and got stoned like high school hoods, and then I played the Barbie board game with M. and T. and T. won (in a cheap dress and a geeky boyfriend, no less!).

Went on to K.'s Birthday party, and it was so packed in the lounge you had to squeeze next to each other to see Kissy Face, another local big fish/little pond drag queen, introduce Kookoo, and wickedly funny Davie Marx did his wickedly funny act, and I fondled little J. in the back, and R.D. smooched me a bit, and of course the true dolphin hunk of my desire, G. C., just smiled.

Another guy started grinning and smiling with me, and we ended up feeling each other up all over, and holding close, and then having a soda and listening to Bobbie Bubble and Kissy Face bitch with Betty, and then B., who I liked, like someone's farm cousin, who is actually the roommate of the guy who slept with my former roommate (small town).

I had the urge to invite B. over as we walked. I dunno. I thought for a minute he might be a bit off, or wanna just rough me up, but I was so wrong. I actually was happy not to play the guest, and the host instead, even though my bed is a mess, but I like to show off my room in its arty sparsity.

So we sat at the kitchen table and chatted and drank water, then I led him in to the bedroom, and like me he was not defined, but sexy, and we nibbled and kissed, and (he didn't suck me!) we did things, and I fucked him three different ways, then he said "Don't come!" and I didn't, then I sat on his dick and he fucked me three ways, then I shot with him in me, and he spewed all over himself.

It was nice, and I slept okay, and I thought I might really like to get to know him, but then he said, just in the darkness, as if some trace of him remained from my bed, and he caught the trail...

"Now I know where I met you. You dated Griffin."

I got out of bed. I had to pee.

I wandered around my apartment while he pretended to sleep. I ducked out on the tiny back porch to eat some fog.

Was there some trace of Griffin somewhere in the house that he'd come to pilfer? Some movement in my body that reminded him? Skin cells? Spit?

The next morning he didn't even ask for my number, which made me disappointed, and put off, but okay about it as well, since he was 24 and young and it was just about the quickest silly thing in a while.

Er, at least, well, it seemed I wasn't going to fuck Griffin out my mind, but I was gonna try.

184-193. What, you say? Well, that's an estimate. The weekend was quite a trip, a sojourn of new sensory experiences.

First, Friday night I stayed in since Harlan never called, that ne'er do well. Just as well. I had a good time at home.

Saturday was having lunch with Joel at the Porch Cafe, realizing I hadn't been there since F. took me there with his ex, J., whom I saw at the bank. We recognized each other, but didn't speak. Hmm.

Anyway, we're at the Porch, and Joel is talking about bondage, and really into preparing for this adventure, and I guess I am too, but I'm being a bit standoffish, cos I'm really not into Joel sexually, but he's great for a fun friend, and I figure, with bondage, it'll be okay.

We make plans for Chett Marks's party that night, disappointing as it is that Ken Jefferson will not be doing us, since he was away in Boston (Ken Jefferson, local handsome bondage god, model to all the great SM stores, the only boy at the gym who can get away with wearing a T-shirt that reads: "FUCK ME... and the horse I rode in on.").

But the fates were kind, and sent us an angel, Hadrian, who met Joel and invited us to P.'s party up in the Berkeley Hills. I was transfixed by Hadrian's boyish beauty, and he oozed a warm sensuality that I wanted very much to be a part of. Not directly. I sensed I probably wouldn't be making love to him, but any of his friends would have been wonderful.

Joel and I parted ways for a bit, then met up later and rode in his car over to Berkeley to check the sunset and meet P., and just generally meet Jean L. and others there. We helped set up, and it was nice seeing things get together. P. (computer whiz program genius) has a split-level pomo house on the edge of a hill overlooking the entire bay, and it was shimmering. The house has lovely plants and glass doors and wooden homey angles.

We said farewell, paid for our X, and saved it, and went back to Joel's for his preps for the bondage party. I had my stuff in a bag in the trunk. Joel shaved his body in the living room, trying to make it an erotic event, but I was more enchanted by Liquid Television, particularly "Eon Flux." I helped him, and regarded his penis piercing with interest, if not a queasy curiosity.

Chett Marks was looking fine in his tattoos and codpiece, being fun and affectionate. He had chains and racks and slings and manacles set up in places through his bare apartment.

Some guys were getting started, but Joel and I were the youngest guys there (except one with a nice chunky frame. I wanted to nibble his butt.) It was all so calm, not at all with the tension I expected, but I kind of expected it to be different, tense. Instead, it was like a lab of SM, a salon.

Joel manacled me to the standing chains, and I dressed in an old t-shirt and the ripped up "Sam Demuth" jeans, called that since I wore them the first time on the day I first had sex with Sam, in a warehouse in Brooklyn. Well, those were in shreds before long. That was fun.

Joel was in his leather gear, and didn't get very nasty, except the sparkings and nipple clamps, which really worked my tits. Maybe I will grow nips, who cares?

Joel got really cock-sucky affectionate humpy with me, but I couldn't get hard. He was being a bad top, getting all mushy. I looked forward to finishing, but then he asked me to get into the sling, which was fun, the clanking sounds and feeling of being raised up nice, especially under the blindfold. My feet were massaged by an older man, who knew I'd lose circulation in my feet, which was an interesting experience in itself, I forget what Joel did to my body, just a little butt probing that made me nervous, also my balls were wrapped in the black shoelaces that Greg at Worn Out West had given me when I bought my new used vest and nip clamps.

I got out of that contraption, and we changed. Joel was a very good bottom. I laid him out on Stan's suspended Gumby rack, and tied his cock to the rope, which I wrapped around him.

I pulled the end of the rope, tugging the whole rack like a hammock by the rope around his erect cock. Joel swung slowly back and forth, the rope connected only to his cock.

I leaned indolently against the far doorway, my cock out, and Chett came up and said, "I had no idea you were such a bad boy."

I returned to Joel's inert body, slapped and pinched and prodded my dildo at his butt, but then some other guys came along to touch Joel and jerk him off, and he came in big clear spurts.

We cleaned up and went on Stuff, or Hump, whatever the nightclub was called that week, wearing disco clothes now, and I veered up to the VIP room, where the usual suspects were holding court; Tabitha, Justin Time (never letting down her Kookoo act), Kent Clark, Miss Judy Jade, Jay and Bri, the usual trash.

Bobby Bubble looked great in his Cookie Monster outfit. All was forgiven, for the moment. Joel tried to score more X, but I didn't care, so I followed him around for a few loops through the club. He wanted to leave for the Berkeley orgy. I was more than ready. We missed the Miss Uranus Pageant totally, but didn't care. We had a party to go to, cocks to suck!

The drive zoomed with some ditsy rave mix Joel had. The entire bay flattened, spreading, a jelly sandwich of *Blade Runner* lights opening wider as we rose the Berkeley hills.

The minute we were back at P.'s we swallowed our X and I danced a bit and enjoyed watching Hadrian in his batik skirt swirl while his slightly chunky ex-swimmer's bod exuded warm boyness. P. was glowing and we hugged and danced and chatted.

Folks were eating and smoking and a big bald lesbian was playing bongos like no tomorrow to the rave beat, which I liked in this party, it wasn't so malevolent like it is in big clubs. Black-haired German Lupo was a terrific DJ, so delicate yet wild in his taste. Hadrian's boyfriend was dancing around shirtless, like a truck driver. Other boys and girls all danced in and out.

I hopped in the hot tub while a few others lay, and Joel had already grabbed onto a guy. The X began to tingle in my belly from the water, so I liked that and after drying off, danced some more.

Later I saw Joel, who came back with the cutest guy, Bruce, and then told me there was non-stop group man sex going on in P.'s bedroom, and I should just join in.

I did in a while, realizing that Hadrian was so happy as is, and there were other adventures to be had.

I crept into a beautifully draped bedroom, like a harem, and five naked men undulating and bobbing away on the bed. They told me to strip and dive in.

"I just want to watch for a while," I said, like a count enjoying his court. I sat on the sofa, then joined in. Bruce was the main guy for me the whole night, but certainly there were others, in interesting and pleasant combinations, but the X helped me relax and let virtually everyone touch me and suck me.

Hours later, there were times when I had to go outside, and I escaped for water or some fruit, only to see that the upstairs had cooled down, and most were off to sleep.

Except Hadrian, and Denton and R., who were an odd trio, didn't seem to be like the others. R. interested me, sort of a lanky stud boy with more in his head than meets the eye, but his friends were obnoxious and kept trying to get me to have sex with them, which I didn't want. It was nice to watch Joel park his small frame atop Denton's immense uncut cock, like a boat, a pontoon of flesh, so amazing I had to slurp on it a while before Joel got down to really riding him.

They joined us downstairs later, but there were so many men, little Will, whom Bruce devoted so much attention to, and K., longhaired and handsome, and some other cute guy who never came down, stirred my thoughts.

But Bruce and I hit it off, and he was the one who consistently got me hard. I can't really stay interested in one body without seeing his eyes, and all Bruce had to do was sit with me and jerk me off to get me stiff.

By morning, everybody had tried everybody else. A few had come, but I hadn't and really wanted to with Bruce, who sat intertwined with me while I finger-fucked his nice chunky ass. He got amazingly hard and I wish he'd have come with me, but I wasn't all that goal-oriented. So I lay back some more, then ended up outside for a while, then ate some fruit, and placed a few pieces of orange slice in a band of sunlight on a pillow near angel Hadrian's sleeping head. His boyfriend served it to him later, which made me feel a twinge of jealousy, but I let it pass, for they were beautiful together.

I went into the bathroom to shower, the water so rusty, and R. came in and peed, asking me to let him suck my cock.

I enjoyed our little bathroom romp, but he wanted me to fuck him right there, on the counter, which made me nervous.

It was fun, slamming it into him while we watched ourselves in the mirror. He was pretty bony too, but really cute. We ejaculated in the sink.

I dried and dressed and went back out on the porch. Chatted outside with a young high school dropout, a speeded up chatty pimple-faced queen and a few others, including an ex-priest who was totally bonkers and majorly informed at the same time, talking about the maharishi gnu age or somebody astrally projecting more pot to them.

I noticed as Locus (Lupo's pale blond longhaired lover) shared a blanket with me, his beautiful eyes captivating, that he had a small scar on his forehead, not unlike the small paint dabble on P.'s head that morning. Were they in a cult? Was I doomed to be brainwashed? Not.

Joel strolled out, glass o' carrot juice in hand, half-dressed, his eyes still twinkling with the spark of X. He must have scored another hit, because I was ready to plant myself on the porch all day and talk stupid philosophy and admire the sunrise.

"You comin'?"

"Where, back home?"

"No, you forgot. I'm picking up my roommate and we're headed to Tahoe."

"No, man, I'm gonna enjoy myself here a while. Think I'll just swim back home."

"Suit yourself."

"I try."

He leaned down and planted a sweet kiss on my cheek before leaving.

Locus and I talked, then R., whom I'd fucked in the bathroom, came outside in a towel, looking like a Bruce Weber. He said he'd give me ride home.

Said goodbye to P., took some carrots for the road (no carrot juice yet, or any of the wonderful breakfast that was being made,) but R.'s car was a totally cool '72 sky blue Charger, old but roomy. Outside I finally got to chat with the incredibly handsome Irving (?) who had on some hot shorts and his legs were thick but he was out of it, spaced to the max with his banter, but we met.

We waited a long time for R.'s friend Denton (obnoxious, drunken, huge dick which I slurped) and some other friend of theirs who must have spent most of his time underneath all the bodies, since I never saw him.

They were both exhausted, thankfully, so R. and I chatted while we drove back. He was a bit out of it, late for work, worried about running out of gas, unable to get something to eat (I sensed a totally twisted thing going on between these guys that I suddenly wanted no part of). He didn't look so much like a Bruce Weber anymore. Well, maybe a bad shot.

He dropped me off and I walked home, rested, then remembered I had a date with Harlan to go to the symphony and see that cute Russian baritone perform. Guzzled coffee to stay awake, but didn't have to, since his voice was so luscious, all the sex and tingles came flooding back and I was in tears.

In one 24-hour period I went from Castro brunch clone to bondage leather stud to rave hippie X-head to working plebe to suit and tie symphony queen!

Quite a weekend, but as Homer Simpson would say, "Must... sleep. Must... sleep."

I hope I meet Bruce and Hadrian and the nice folk from that party again. The way things spontaneously work so much better than forced good times should be a reminder. You can't make things like this happen. They just happen.

194. Rode to Black Sands Beach. Laid out and enjoyed it all, then cruised the little rocky glen and found a guy right off.

"Wanna jack off?" I asked.

He was built good, not great, but had a nice smile and arty glasses, and as we tugged our black bathing suits down to let our cocks out another guy came up, but I wasn't up for him, reddish blond. I jacked the guy and bit his nips and bent over to suck him, and he did the same to me. Enjoyed it, but we didn't finish, he said let's take a break. So later, after sunning and swimming more, I hiked up to a nice cliff and jacked off looking out over the bay.

198. Big day. Rose had a flat. Took the human-powered bike, Nishiki. Went riding through Golden Gate Park, then cruised Land's End. Saw a few good prospects, including a thin boy with a big dick, it seemed, hanging down in his shorts, but he never held still long enough for me to get him.

Others, many others, strolled by, more faunlike Filipinos and nondescript men. I went all the way up a high rock to check out a skinny guy, who didn't seem so hot up close.

But I laid out above him, let him pass by then jacked off for his visual delight while he hid in the trees, another guy watching and jacking off from above.

I didn't come, tired by it all, and quickly laid down, showing off my butt. Nice sunning.

Hiked around, then went to Baker Beach, but didn't go down to the beach because a guy was just sitting by his little red car, long blond hair, black sweats, sunglasses, no shirt, big furry pecs.

Just a few looks and he went off into the shrubs.

I followed.

We went into a bunker, but he asked me if I wanted to go to another place, where we found a glen, quiet, and private and stripped down. He made out slowly, tastily. He was older, maybe forty and chunky in a good way. We jacked real slowly, and fingered each other's butts slowly, and really sucked deep and slow, and held off coming for the longest time never even laid down, just did it in various creative ways to fit the slant of the ground. Mushroomy head. He really spewed.

At his car, he hesitantly gave me his number. He was married to someone, the ring on the finger. Duh. Gave me his office number. Like I'll call a cheater.

200. Saw The London Suede at Slim's with Harlan. Good show, really good show. Liked the band. They got me all horny and romantic at the same time. I know, I know, when will I ever learn. These men that claim to be spiritual have their groins in one room and their hearts in the other, the kitchen, in the freezer, no doubt.

I guess it was time to thaw.

Was feeling antsy, knew it, since I wore my GI Joe dog tags and my Trojan socks, so something was in the air (or my pants.) Harlan didn't want to go to a bar, and so he walked home with another friend who we met up with at the club, said it was okay, since I wanted to have cheap sex, which Harlan doesn't do, so I went to That Place, and chatted with a friend of a friend, and checked out the alley, where several not so hot guys were pants-down doing it. Drank my beer and left.

Rode to The Cock Factory and N., who worked coat check, got me in free. Thanks. Didn't take more than two minutes before I spotted a hot mustachioed bald daddy with major bod and light blond fur.

Who could ask for anything more? We got a booth and hugged and rubbed and licked and kissed, and dropped our drawers. I knelt to suck him, and he was uncut! but didn't get hard, and didn't suck me, but I didn't mind, since he was such a good kisser, we hugged and humped groins and I spat pecker snot against his belly and he lifted me up off the ground and it felt good. We laughed afterward. I chatted with N. at the clothes check, and saw two actor types I knew come in and figured that was enough.

201-202. J. and Denton and B.'s party. After the beach, in which I got to talk with cute little R. It was nice. Then rushed home to get into leather, since it was called a leather party, a mistake, since I was immediately separated from the vanilla types. But I played with a cute tall guy's ass for a bit in the dungeon, the dirt floor under the house in the back yard with black plastic hung down in faux-rooms. Initiated the play by going at a guy roped up, who everyone wanted to touch. Then later, J. got in his sling and I really went to town on him, then others helped, then two drunken queens shoved in, but I got them out of the way.

Took J. in the dungeon area, and said "There's something I've been wanting to do with you for months, a sacrament of sorts."

I got him on his knees and peed in his mouth. It was great, transcendent. We got the drunken queens out and got into the bathroom. J. and I then peed on each other in the shower. He finger-fucked me and I jerked off standing, we showered. Denton, his roommate, came in wearing boxers. While he got his saline solution, I watched his crotch. His dick peeked out of his shorts.

Back in his bed, J. fucked me a bit. I came. Then he tried to come but couldn't, a little exhausted, I think. I left the next morning, feeling like trash. I think I've had enough of this leather thing.

203. Wandered around the Castro Pink Party for hours. Saw many men, mostly strangers. Had a beer with B., who danced outrageously at Cafe San Marcos. Ran into R. from P.'s Berkeley orgy. He reminded me that he worked in a hair salon right in the Castro. We went to his salon and he blew me on a barber chair with hundreds of homos screaming and hooting in the street below. I think some people could even see us.

Then I tentatively agreed to take him home, and it felt good, even though he's a bit odd, with his hair and odor fetish, he's a good fuck, and I drilled him.

The next morning he jerked me off while rimming me. I felt odd with him. I thought he was positive, but more important, he was ... I don't know, jaw-drop gorgeous and strange. I get antsy when I see that glint of Griffin, that sex demon thing, and I don't have room for that.

205. Denton and I went to Black Sands beach, compelled there. Denton was having "marital problems." I still couldn't shake the occasional pangs of fear when I saw a guy who slightly resembled Griffin. We needed escape and we got it.

Boys were doing it all over. Spent all day, running around, playing with guys, flirting, chatting, watching a herd of naked men watch two stupid guys climb up the wrong cliff and spill rocks. Watched Denton make out with a tall Swiss guy in the cave, then later ran around.

Talked with a really cute big-nosed, longhaired muscle guy with a great butt.

Saw him looking at me in the little klatch, either critically or appraisingly, but looking at my torso and dick for a while.

Never got his name or closer, but later, nude, jacked off and sucked with Steven, from Northern England, who knew the Swiss that Denton was later entangled with on the beach. Seeing the two of them 69 was nice. Seeing Denton sucking on such a huge cock was nice. We both had some lovely easy beach sex to get our minds off the bastards who broke our little codependent hearts.

206. Went to Boner Vista Park at 7:30. Duskier, nice. Sat in a tree like a leopard and watched the oceanside view, then back to the gay part across from the apartment building and passed an older guy, definitely a possibility, since younger guys are usually skittish.

Glad I wore my boots. By the time he came down from above me along the path, I'd already played tingly with myself, pissing just a tiny trickle at a time, and got hard. Older guy had a mustache and jacked me, then leaned over and sucked me. I jacked him and the uncut thing became a monster, and quite clean as I slogged its immensity into my gullet.

I really had to pee, and that sometimes forces the come out faster, but he knelt and sucked more, then jacked me while I sat/leaned against a jutting tree root. I spewed, then helped him get off, and then we joked and chatted. He was Steffan, from Germany, and visiting and going to live in New York.

He kept spitting out drool after sucking me, like he didn't even want to risk tasting me. Odd.

Walked home through the park as the skyline glowed with just a mysterious trace of light in the sky. Several darkly-dressed strange men appeared, including one who dressed himself in complete blackness behind a shrub. It seemed the perfect time to leave.

207, 208, 209. Went to Seattle to visit with B. and G., his man. Had an odd time. We went camping out at Triangle Campground, a private gay place by a river, like a lowkey Fire Island.

At the Mardi Gras party, I went dressed as an Egyptian guy, outdone by muscley hunks in expensive headdresses, flowing white capes and harem pants. Stripped it off after a while, inverted my headdress back to the T-shirt it was.

Ended up going with two guys in leather jackets to their campground. They kept wanting to have sex standing up by the fire, which made me think they wanted to show off, or for a friend in the tent, or on a camera somewhere. Anyway, I got tired of it, didn't really need to fuck or be fucked, or was so fagged out from all the pot I couldn't keep up. The older guy was like a nice army sergeant, the younger a soft pup in blond hairs. After we fucked, I peed in the fire and it hissed.

210. Back in SF, Denton was back with Vic, who had a friend named Mick, who went with us to the Eagle, and after getting drunk, we went to The Cock Factory for a cock dunk.

I know, the meter's off, but hey.

I had no idea it was open so early on Sunday, and then I knew why. It was boring. There were so few men I wanted to touch, let alone suck. Mick was all into it, being a total sex pig. I finally saw a porno tape I liked, so I wandered up to the racks, a sort of dick trough, stuck my noodle through a slot and felt a wet mouth play with me. I spat my juice watching a leather muscle stud on TV do the same. Yawn.

Harlan invited us over to watch *And the Band Played On*. Later we watched Mystery Science Theater 3000 and I tried not to show how happy I was to see Harlan take off his pants, me laying in his bed with him.

I couldn't keep my eyes off Harlan's crotch. He kept reaching down in his shorts to scratch his dick or balls, and one time his dick just flopped down on his belly. I will never forget that moment. It was so frustrating being in bed with him, and playing, and wrestling, and slapping his bubble butt, and us not having sex. I could be happy having sex with these two for the rest of my life, but they're my only friends and it's very important to keep friends, but I can't help wondering if the only reason I stay with them is the remote possibility that they will someday, somehow let me into their beds.

Sometimes I think I should just cut it off and become a castrati.

212. Back in New York for work fun; a journalists' convention. Went with a colleague to a bar, and he said he wanted to find some "action."

"Hop on," I said as I led him to a cab.

We started at Tunnel Vision, got high with Scotty and his oddly attractive friend, then Bijou 82 for a bit of show it off, then grab a guy and get off. My colleague was stunned, having never been to a sex club, but was soon enveloped in a cocksucking fourway before I'd even gotten him a beer. It was the dress shirt and tie that lured them in.

I found other fun.

He was muscled, but older and bad skin, but sucked okay, then sat on my lap and jacked me in a fake fuck. Nice. Sex for the first time in months, and I only had to fly 3,000 miles to get it.

Visited J., who moved into my dilapidated apartment in the East Village. Packed stuff up that I had stored in the closet for too long, including some art, rare first editions books, some fave porno mags (Cole Carpenter spewing, that PR stud who danced naked before me at the Gaiety). Shipped them off to California. Pretty, petty, pity. Was I ever returning for good?

Back in SF, February something. Got stoned after work and went riding my bike around, ended up way down at the docks, jacking off by a pier. a guy in a car came up, and another guy kept walking by at the pier by some tugboats, suspicious. I went off to a place behind a truck and jacked off against its rear tire.

K. B. invited me to an orgy.
He kept me in the dark about it for a long time, but after reading DOGZ, he seemed interested, and it sounded like a fun story idea.
But then his partner, one of them, Denton somebody, called, and invited me up to his place for "pizza and wine," very relaxed supposedly. It wasn't.
Very nice, swank *apartemente* near Buena Vista, high up, great living room view. Another guy was there, L. Cute, from back east. He's a performer, it happens. Promises of pleasure. I definitely wanted him.
R., the host was weird, didn't even offer to take my coat. After hiking all the way up the hill, I had to ask for water.

Anyway, these guys are trying to sell me on this silly orgy as a feature article (the gay magazine staff would blanche, I explained. What about Drummer?), and I can tell it's gonna be a real pretentious set up. They talk about theatricality, and all I'm thinking is, they just invited me because I can write, and all the guys are gonna be buff and no one, no one is gonna wanna touch me.

It's most unpleasant, these awkward, distant feelings about sex that cloud my brain. No one asks me out. I meet no one. I go out and get re-introduced to the same bunnies over and over again, and now, when they find out where I work, they always have a comment. I'm still thinking about quitting, but then the Publisher gives me this pension packet, like now I'm in the family, and whee, I'm supposed to be happy, but it's just dug me further into this and I find it even harder to think about what I would do to get out nd go back to New York.

I'd been trying to get buff for this orgy, the Bacchanalia Club, catchy name, like I'm doomed to write about it, eh?

Aside from the fact that this R. guy is slimy as all get out, the odd way he talked about "being into Black men now" made me want to ask about Latinos and Asians too, like, Are you "into them" now, too?

But it was so odd, the way he had this elegant table set and we ate cheesy pizza, with forks. Empty wine glasses. K. didn't eat. It was odd. I kept sitting silently, amazed by their persistence in pitching the damn thing. I mean, the orgies I've enjoyed all just happened. They weren't so forcibly created.

So, the cherry on it all was when R. gets out his photos from his Phoenix Hotel party, this big gay faux-Palm Springs bash, mentioning one cute guy after another, who's gonna be there, and of course there was a picture of him, smiling devilishly, in a Speedo, his lithe body out in the sun for anyone to enjoy: Griffin.

"He's gonna be there?" I asked.

"Sure," he said.

I excused myself to take a shit.

The Pup of pups was invited too. It was inevitable, I should have known.

I sat in the well-appointed can, watching the paisley wallpaper swirl, and wondered what the hell I was gonna do in a room with him, naked and supposed to have a good time with sex, with him, who drive me nuts with his constant reminder that I would never have him again, he who cut me off with one phone call, that single hang-up, me who cut him off so stupidly, he who introduced me to a life of closeness and such sexual wildness, and what was I supposed to do if I saw him having sex with some guy or a bunch of guys? Watch?

Of course I would want to watch. I would want to see him hard, his cock sliding in and out of some guy's mouth or butt or both, see him riding some porn stud, and maybe touch him just to make him mad, or just watch him all night to ruin his evening, or just lean over and go "boo."

Maybe I would call him and say, "I'm gonna be at that orgy tonight, I thought I'd tell you so in case that makes you uncomfortable, you can make other plans."

But then I think, how many others will be there that know me, that slight me, that think so little of me? How long can I hide out from these men, deny the hell of this life, while all the while supposedly fighting for our right to live it?

My body ached from trying to be muscular. My evenings were lonely, and lonelier still when I worked out, or dove into anonymous "forget him" sex, felt like such a non-body while I try to make a body or love a body.

I could already feel the guys trying me out, then getting bored because I don't have big tits or thick arms, wondering the whole time if they would secretly videotape the whole thing. I felt, when I was talking to the producers of this orgy, that I was in about to be drafted into the clutches of something graciously evil.

I had to show my cards. Days later, I told K. about my predicament, but he said I should just deal with it, and probably enjoy it if I just "avoid him like the plague."

But I can't avoid the plague, and I wanted, at one time, to risk the plague just to have his love. Will they try to steer me away if I want to be near Griffin, hover close and threaten him sexually?

Home again, confused by the invitation, I found some no-sun tanning oil and slathered some on as a test. I thought of that Pet Shop Boys song, "Do you want to forgive her, or do want revenge?"

215 - 227. (Yup. Twelve)

I was nervous, and gulped a glass of wine while ironing my shirt. ridiculous, since it ended up in a plastic bag with all my other clothes as soon as I got there.

The mansion was huge, a stately pushed back house in the Western Addition, hidden in its beauty. L. greeted me at the door in his undies.

It was huge and dark, a foyer fit for the Addams Family. K. greeted me at the entrance to the basement, where our clothes were stored by a not-too-friendly clothes-check boy. Beyond the closet room, two men were playing on a huge console, stereoware out of *Star Trek*.

The sound system, in a side hallway, blinked and glowed with layers of green and red dots and wave forms. Already guys were arriving. awkwardly lining up for the bathroom, sipping beers and bumming smokes in the kitchen. The videos were playing some serious fisting stuff, which caused most to make jokes. "I hope we don't have to see any more of that!"

At 11ish, most had gathered in the main living room area, which was lined with black bean bag chairs and a floor of black padding. It became the sort of kiva, and groups of friends chatted and giggled in amused anticipation.

Oh yes, I knew many, at least by sight. What was wonderful was that it was such a social atmosphere, for those brave enough to chat and open up. Others were still nervous, clutching their skimpy white towels, didn't know anyone, or were playing it cool. It was hard to tell the difference between snobbery and shyness, at first. Griffin was nowhere in sight. Relief. Disappointment.

Our hosts, dressed in black robes and masks, entered amid tolling bells, announced the Bacchanal open, and like a slo-mo starter's pistol, began playing for us to watch, then crawling over to the sidelines, where my bud Joel, who lay in my lap as I massaged him, got the first of the evening's treats.

Things progressed smoothly, and I ended up in a lovely four-way with an ultra-cute acquaintance from the gym who I knew was a dancer, he appreciated my calf-licking as much as the cock stuff.

I had to pee from the beer, and walked up the huge stairs, hardon sinking as I tread up the stairs to the john, where two boys were in the shower.

I ended up doing some fun rimming with David, a little Asian, and hauling him up on my hips for all to see. I love those portable men.

Segue: traveling around, going into the front room, where things were tighter. A few really muscular guys ruled the central area, with offshoots enjoying the sights. Kept bumping into boners and pumping hands. I fortunately ended up straddled behind the beefiest, furriest guy there, who enjoyed my slurping his sweaty smooth back, furry steeled tits and sumptuous ass while he butt-surfed, then got a condom, and fucked another big guy. I humped from behind, wanting to fuck him too, but he kept reaching back to grab it and guide it up, butt surf style. Sometimes I ducked down to lap at his balls as they slid back and forth. It was primo.

In the little changing room where everyone had stripped down, things got exciting as I stumbled over, then into, porn actor Bill Marlowe, whose sucking and shrimping of a hugely hung blondie was made everso more savory as he shared the prong with me, then moved on to the other huge hunk. I poked his ass with my finger while being impaled by this man thing. Fireworks. I love to shoot while choking on it.

Relaxed, smoked a joint on the back porch with a guy, who I would later get off. We talked about a three-way fuck, but I didn't do that.

Followed some humpy ones around, a Latino with a huge everything, but he was sampling everybody, poking his cock in crotch-level mouths. Another one, an inflated Marky Mark, was doing the same, but smiled as I appreciated his tits and ass. Marvelous cock.

Got a dorky guy off on a bean bag. He was a little too pushy; "Do this, Do that." A little funny attitude in the hot tub. Porn boy and some other guy got next to me, but not to be friendly, to shove me aside to make room for their underwater jack off action.

Went back into the changing sofa room, where L. was kneeling before Immense Hunk #2, who was smooching with another big hunk, who was also getting sucked off. I sidled up behind L. and held and fondled him while he went to town. Watched him suck, and watched the big porn look-alike ejaculate, then L. leaned into me and came. Hooray. Quite a sight. Awkward chatting afterward.

A small, beautiful Black guy, shaved head, got enthusiastic and fucked me. Poked and hurt a bit, but it was nice. Still couldn't really get it off, too many guys around us, jacking off and watching. Too much. They liked the way my cock danced, though, upside down, as he fucked me.

We showered with about three other guys in a giant shower room, each of us playing around with our butts and dicks. Soapy.

Dressed, said goodnight to K., lost L., but hope to see him again.

Altogether, an awkward night, yet fun. Some attitude, but no more than the usual. I feel like it's a lesson, but as K. and I discussed, it's not a place to find intimacy, but I could have, if I'd been attracted to the guys who liked me. I felt the imbalance, the power play of biggest getting serviced by smaller, and others hovering around the perimeter. I wasn't sure where I stood.

Riding home, though, I couldn't help but wonder if Griffin deliberately didn't show up, if he'd heard I'd be there, if he had shown, the fireworks that could have transpired, the performance, the reunion of our bodies

228. Some kind of impulse demanded similar behavior a week later. I got stoned with M. at lunch, then took off walking down Folsom, pretending I was just going for some unusual lunch, and went to the Folsom Gulch (Full Cum Gulp) and popped into the booths and there was a huge, huge, longhaired, muscled Native American stud. Whoa, beginner's luck.

I walked right to a buddy booth, and didn't lock the door, and he followed me in.

"Is this okay?" I asked.

"Sure. You not from here?"

"Just haven't done this here."

I started by fondling his immense brown chest, then his gargantuan arms, then licking his hard pillow of biceps, then he pulled up his shirt and I sucked his titties, grazed down to his stomach and then up his chest. He was brown and warm and smelled funky, but not too much. He hauled out his wiener, which hung down a good four inches, then I played with it, and sucked his balls while he whacked. Shit. It's gonna happen.

There was a clatter of doors after us, guys hoping to see on the window side or something. I fished out my dick and jacked, then he got hard and shoved it in, sometimes slamming it down my gullet, then taking a break, then letting me lick around.

I stood and we nestled and humped dicks, then I turned and he played with my ass and pumped his cock at my hole, on it but not in it.

His fist kept humping, rubbing against my bung. Then I turned and lowered again and he face-fucked me some more. I slurped the head at breaks and slathered up and down slow, but he loved banging, and he banged away.

He damn near fucked the snot out of my skull.

I was mucousy and ready to pop.

But then he said, "Gotta take a break." I wanted his jizz all over me, mine all over his legs, but I let him go. He kissed me, deep tongue stuff, then left.

I pumped off in the booth, savoring the taste of him, the smell he left in the booth. My come splattered all over the wall.

I shucked my pants up and about a dozen guys watched me as I left. One guy darted in. I imagined him licking the walls. I nodded at the Native stud, then walked out into the bright sunshine and had a huge meatball sandwich for lunch.

231, 232

Piss-fucked a guy while he sucked another guy's cock whose ass I'd licked in a previous position.

In the back of a FedEx truck.

Were I a poet, I would have stopped there, but I'm not, so let's continue. How did I get in the back of the FedEx truck to begin with?

Some downtown 1015 circuit party failed me after a few hours, so I put my pants back on and walked past, a few other bars along Folsom.

A parking lot by the packaging service intrigued me because the fence was open. The lighting, an amber streetlight, fencing; *West Side Story* meets early Falcon.

I wandered around looking for a place to piss or jack off and then fondled the FedEx truck and noticed it wasn't locked in the back. So of course I pulled it up with a rumble and got in.

There were no packages, of course. The back end was completely wooden blank. I stood around, strutting, trying to eroticize the space and it's containment.

It wasn't exactly working, but I was gonna give it a go. The cab was locked, so it was just the back space.

After a while, I noticed a car pull up the fence in the next parking lot, stopping right in front of the FedEx truck.

I could see through the front window that they were quietly discussing something, then smoking a joint. I was almost in a panic, but thought they could be sort of an unknown audience for me, so I continue to stroke myself.

Then they got out of the car and slowly walked out, then into my parking lot. I slowly lowered the truck tailgate, then considered just sitting on the flatbed.

As they spotted me, one of them seemed disappointed while the other was intrigued. They approached slowly and blunt greetings were exchanged.

"Wanna get in?" the bold one said, impatient to get things started.

We each trundled up together. At first, I just watched the two guys kiss, until one explained that they were boyfriends just having fun. That sounded good.

I sort of watched for a while until one of them grabbed for my dick and then things got connected; dicks to mouth, fingers to butts, tongues in armpits.

At one point, top boy proved his status and started probing between the butt cheeks of his boyfriend, who leaned over as he sucked me a bit too voraciously.

Bottom boy took a break, dug in his pocket and took out some lube, soaping up his dick and his butt hole. I stood watching, waiting until top boy started thrusting in and out, and then after a few pounding minutes offered a nod and a finger toward his rear end. I was game.

So basically, I was lapping top boy's jiggling balls and licking his butthole between thrusts, until he arched back and shoved his ass back, my face deeper, my tongue digging into his anus, until he sped up to yank out his load. I missed his spurts, despite trying, instead licked his bottom's back.

Despite not be able to stay exactly hard, both bottom boy I felt an obligation to hurry up and finish because it was all too terrific.

Bottom boy compensated by persisting to pump as his boyfriend slowly teased his spent cock over his lips.

But cum was not coming for him. So top boy grabbed my hips and encouraged me to try to fuck his boyfriend. He was bit too moist and sloppy and I couldn't stay exactly hard, so I just relaxed, then asked politely, taking their wide-eyed zeal as approval, and then pissed up his ass.

It absolutely positively delivered.

233- lost count. Bacchanalia #2.

It didn't help to have J. at the door, a dorky "model" who I'd attempted to date a few times, but broke it off, saying I needed to just stop the sex thing altogether for a while. J. was catty the moment Lee and I got in.

"Well, it looks like you're back in circulation."

"Quite."

What the hell was that prude doing greeting people for an orgy? Like having a Mormon at the door of a speakeasy.

Porno boy who I'd sucked off at the last orgy sat across from him in a leather mask gear, his collar chained to the wall.

"Trash, trash, trash," some other queen joked, while I fumbled with my helmet to find my invite.

Lee and I walked in awkwardly. We'd also invited tattooed dude Eric, whom I danced with a while, and N., who sort of trotted about in a fab Gautier-type vest, which a friend made for him. Lee and I had come totally overdressed.

By the time we got there, guys were dancing in nothing but little white towels, and ready to go. Lots of bods, but I couldn't focus on anyone, wanted to, but the pot we'd smoked was too trippy.

I was entranced by K, the burly muscled Black dancer, whom I'd only showered with at the previous orgy. He danced nearly naked across the floor. I think he was looking at me.

Despite the Leather theme, the chaps and shirt were useless, so I stripped those off as I danced. Wanted to toss the fucking chaps, I hated them so, they were so dumb, but I settled for ripping off the shiny black T-shirt that Griffin had left behind somewhere a long time ago when we'd thought of playing dress-up. Figured it would be my sacrifice to the gods.

A semblance of a "show" commenced in the middle of the large living room.

We stood watching, realized it wouldn't get going just yet, then eventually got up to the clothes check.

I stripped down to my black shorts with the funny little lace up front that Harlan gave me oh so long ago in New York, then realized everyone wore nothing but towels, so like a dream gym class, I donned mine near rows of paper bags of clothes. I trod back up to the lounge fuck space, which was going full tilt.

Met up with M.D., and we smooched, then this tall furry leather dad got up behind me and wasted no time slapping on a rubber and discovering the joys of my ass. I wasted no time finally getting it from both ends, standing up, something I've always wanted to try, ever since that scene in *Stryker Force*. Thankfully my back was in a good mood or I would have been dragged out of there on a gurney.

I sucked and kissed with M.D., had to let the leather top stop, what was really nice was watching he and M.D. kiss right in front of me. Wow.

I got down on the floor with M. and he sucked me, then, my gift from the gods, a huge, burly burnished blond muscle dad, knelt down beside me and clamped mouths with me. We smooched for a long time.

I politely told M.D. I'd be back to him. He was cool with that and got some other attention while I maneuvered around with the lion-like behemoth and did some major face-sucking.

It was odd, all those legs around us, like that Tom of Finland cartoon with the nude guy lying down and all those legs around him.

Problem was all those legs were attached to tweaking queens who couldn't see our hands, and we got more than a bit stepped on among the bean bags and them losing their balance.

But it was worth it, and fun, feeling so low down trashy. Lying comfortably while they all struggled to remain erect, and erect.

The muscle dad Lion King was like a vinyl salt lick, but wouldn't yet let me go to town on him. He just laid me down, we humped groins and he sucked my neck, sucked my little chain and lock, then opened his jaw, and I swear, just like those nature films, was gonna suck the blood out of me right there, right for the jugular. "LeStat," I whispered to myself. "You've been working out."

I was ready for it, I could have become his love slave, the way he growled, but then we had to sit up for a breather, and I lavished my hands over his mounds of muscle and gut. Wonderful.

He said he probably wouldn't be getting hard, because of his X. I said that was okay. I wasn't really thinking dick time. There was so much else of him.

But then he nestled over me and licked and pawed, and then I asked him to lay on his belly.

I made love to his back, pressing and massaging and licking, watching joyously while he chowed down on a nearby boner.

Me and the guy getting sucked stared into each other's eyes, connected by the Lion King's body. His face was calm with pleasure, nodding his head to the force of the lion below him, head bobbing up and down, my hands shoving him forward as I shoved my fingers in and out of him.

Me and the guy the Lion was sucking both leaning in closer, near kissing, closer, until some guy behind us who'd been pumping his cock while watching blew an arc of sperm between us. It landed on Lion king's butt. I rubbed it in, then rubbed my hand off on his thigh.

I kept staring at my third partner as our muscle stud humped below us. Sure, that guy had his mouth, but I had everything else.

I pawed his ass and smacked it, and he wiggled his gargantuan rump in appreciation, then I wet my fingers and dug in for real and tickled his crevasse, fingering his ass wall, the top, the nub on the bottom. It was way too funky, like he'd come straight from the gym without bathing, but the X must have oozed from his pores into his sweat, cos I was tripping on the taste.

Then we rolled around and giggled and sucked face some more. I liked his beard. He began sucking my cock, no, eating my cock, and I knelt down under him, then my head beside his mountainous thigh, and fingered his hole big time, fucking his endless ass with two fingers. He was finally stiff, and I backed my head down to nestle between his legs.

I got so hard feeling the back of his throat, my cock head banging against his gullet, and his sloshing down into mine, that I shot globs up into him. I had cued him, he knew I was coming, but he gulped it down readily. I would have done the same for him, had he wanted it.

We sat up, and recovered. I licked my come out of his mouth.

"You should have told me," he said.

"Sorry. I wouldn't have done it if I was positive. I was just so excited."

"It's not that," he said. "I wanted you to fuck me."

It was just as well. The condoms were nowhere in sight. Besides, too many people had been watching us the whole time. Any more and we should have been paid.

We tried to talk, but he was standing against the wall, watching the herd go by, and wanting another round with something bigger, no doubt.

For a fragment of a high moment, he was Harlan if he could add fifty pounds of muscle and live to be forty.

I hope he lives to see fifty. In the middle of an orgy, I was thinking of Harlan's health.

Alright. I've had my bliss, now I can't even speak to you, I thought to the muscle guy as we stood together. We parted. He said his name, something Italian. "I hope we meet again," I said, but knew the gods were not that kind.

They were nice enough to let me bump into M.D. downstairs. I shoved a ripe apple slice in his mouth and we chatted on the disco steps, watching the near-empty dance floor as two naked couples on two different levels danced slow, kissing and grinding under tunnels of light.

M.D. and I got campy right off, which I loved, him having a sense of humor about the whole thing. We met his friend, who had come twice - "That's it for me. How much sex does anybody need, after all?"

We met up with Lee, whom I told where I'd be hanging out, even though he seemed a bit lost in it all.

M.D. and I danced and jacked each other, nearly alone on the floor. It was nice. We could have finished there, but wanted to get more comfy.

I saw K. and K., the popular daddy/son couple. I will always want the younger one, especially after playing with uptight daddy K., his lover, at the previous orgy, but hey, some things are not meant to be, so M.D. and I went upstairs.

He sat on me and I sucked him, and then he came on my chest. The TV glare was yucky, and when I stretched out, I bumped a guy in the head.

It was Joel, one bean bag over, and suddenly everyone seemed to be finishing, or doing fine. Chatty hour.

K. the muscley Black dancer, walked by, his big black body glowing in the tube light, his cock jutting forward like a coat hook.

"Anyone got any lube?" he called out, his boner ready. I wondered whose butt lay winking in anticipation.

I asked M.D. if he wanted to go on a date.

"Like a date date?"

"Yeah."

Ridiculous to try it at an orgy, but hey, call me romantic.

"The act of sex, per se, can never be bad;
the uses to which it is occasionally put,
however, certainly can be."
— Scott O'Hara

23

"You've got hepatitis."

The nurse told me bluntly, while I fought to remain sitting upright in the tiny examination room.

"Which one?"

"A and B."

My eyes had turned the sick yellow of the sky on fog-coated nights, my limbs heavy as rocks, my piss thick and chunky, almost with a crystalline discharge. I was fucked up. Sick as a dog.

As if I didn't know.

I'd figured my exhaustion from my last trip from New York was more than just jet lag. Was it the butt I licked after dancing at Roxy? Was it the cock I sucked after carousing the Bar? Perhaps the boy I fucked at Bijou 82. Maybe the twelve chosen at that last orgy? Whoever, it was all a blur.

The one person I knew I didn't get it from, or give it to, was Curt Darby, the boy man of my New York passions.

Ever unrequited lust, he embodied all the boyish joy of a handsome neurotic gay man fearing turning thirty. The two nights we'd been gone out together, he ended up in some other guy's arms. It saddened me to see such joy, that which did not include me.

For two days I lay in bed, getting up only to shit or attempt eating. My hair was a greasy matted mess. I had a jug of water and jars of juices and a pee bowl, since getting up made me so dizzy. I avoided checking myself in the mirror, the jaundice so sickening. I didn't leave the house. Lee and Harlan came over to bring thin soups in Mason jars.

I began to feel a closeness with death, like the dread of an endless tunneled subway ride. At least I might have a seat, since I couldn't stand. The potential for death never seemed so real. I tried to curse someone, something, but I couldn't find the strength.

I hated my body, despised its vulnerability. My cock repulsed me. I thought I would never get another erection again. The thought of sex made me nauseous.

By the middle of the second week, I'd grown tired of my SF apartment, too many smells and sounds. "Gotta try and shake off this creeping malaise," I told myself, now talking aloud while alone.

I ventured out and walked, carefully, not too far, to Duboce Park, where in the warm sun and cheering breeze, I sat at the bench, watching the people play with their dogs. It seemed so cheerful, the relationship. I wondered if Griffin had truly meant what he'd said, about wanting to continue with our games, and I wondered if I had, would he still be with me?

Filled with sun and fresh air, I walked home, more energy in my steps, and resolved to follow more primal routes to my healing. I collected all the loose pages of the zine, the Photostats, and the photos and the negatives, and gathered them in a cluster in my metal trash can. On the back porch, in the bright slat of afternoon light, I poured some lighter fluid on the pile and lit it, watching the painful evidence of him curdle into black flakes.

For the next year I wouldn't drink alcohol, doctor's orders, with the exception of a glass of champagne at New Year's. I had to celebrate something, even if the new life I was determined to create excluded what may have been the one great love of my life.

But there can be no long life in such a man. You can't read a favorite book by the light of fireworks. You can't make a home, find a path, with a maker of labyrinths.

24

"It's all just a little village," Lee had said of the scene. I thought of the tiny puppet land in the 1964 World's Fair, "It's a Small World After All" ringing in my head. I'd seen marionettes at a garage sale a while back, just like the ones I'd collected as a kid, and almost bought them, but the Mexican stereotype was beyond amusing. Maybe I could dress them up more realistically, home boys with little ski caps, or AIDS service group office wear. I decided to pass. Besides, the puppets were really sad.

Leaving the puppets, the impulse buy wouldn't go away, so I went to Safeway and bought salami, Ben and Jerry's Chunky Monkey, and votive candles. I knew, no matter how stupid I'd feel, or how desperate I'd look, I'd end up hitting on some guy if I went out, anyone to help me delete file on everything.

The streets were moist with a brief rain, shiny. The air was thick with mist. I would make a lair for one before leaving forever, but if, just in case, I saw someone worth bringing home, I would be prepared. That always helped.

Well, it used to. How to go back to the dance, savoring the space between the sharing of phone numbers and the first date, full of potential and devoid of regret. How to return to a slow tango when I've been rutting with bucks and bulls, and then cancelled, branded, diseased.

Just a little village.

I could greet guys and know they'd only recently broken up with others guys. They had the same look that was caught in my eyes. Some knew Griffin. Some people who hated me were best friends with people he liked. It seemed the sport was to remain as iron cool as possible, while others might know that a screaming match and bitch fight was expected.

In discussing these flat loops of conversations, where the connection of lust and friendship stops, Harlan put it best: "We will always treasure you for your casual disregard."

We were at a party. Lee had ridden with me. It was one of Bobbie Bubble's enormous blow-outs, with a full cast, crowded into his enormous house on the Avenues.

To show his forgiveness, Bobbie had called me, leaving a message with an invite and the address.

Maybe he was one of the only people in this fog-coated town not to hold a grudge. Maybe he just wanted to stage another catfight.

It was easy to find the place, the only crowded windows and porch among the ghostly streets of this part of San Francisco. No cable cars here, no Victoriana, just row after row of silent homes, nestled next to each other like mausoleums.

The club kids, the pretty boys, the funny radical dykes, the post-hippies and drag queens. There was no need for a guest list. They were all there to pay tribute for the many nights when they were on the guest list. It was like those parties on *Laugh-In,* where everyone had a snappy line.

Some cute guy told me he thought my goatee was really hot, like a true biker dude. He said it with an air that I felt sure was a sarcastic insult. I said thanks and walked away.

I was sitting out on the porch, exhausted by the barrage of quips and lines, the smoky air, when I saw him enter.

Griffin.

I figured if I walked up through the second floor, I'd be able to make my way down the stairs and outside just as he was pushing in through the living room. He'd never see me.

"Well, I'm freezing and out of chit chat," I said to Lee. "You wanna go?"

"Sure," Lee said, but then had a soft whisper with the guy he'd met who had his arms wrapped around my friend.

The thought of parading through that group crowding the living room made me uncomfortable. "Let's go upstairs."

"Is there a door?" Lee asked.

"I think it's locked," Lee's friend said.

"Oh, shit." I fumbled with the lock, then saw the light on in Bobbie's bedroom. His window faced the upstairs porch.

"Let's just go in the window."

"Are you going?" Lee's friend asked.

Lee deftly tossed "I'm gonna stay" into my ear. I blurted an okay while realizing it was sink or swim time. The frame rattled as I pulled it open. Half a dozen people stood around and sat on the bed in Bobbie's room watching a porno tape. They all gasped. The drag queen sitting inside on the bed screeched. Three snow domes fell off the window ledge and out onto the patio.

"You broke them!"

I sighed, picked them up. One leaked water and snow. "It's not as if they're an endangered species."

I sat on the bed, glanced back through the window at Lee, who was curling up with his friend in the darkness. Can I feel happy for him and want to claw him at the same time, I wondered.

"Oh, I know you," said the drag queen.

"Really?"

"You work for that magazine that used my picture without asking." I didn't bother to tell her I'd soon be leaving the magazine. That crunchy bit of gossip had already been raked over the scene's bonfire coals.

"You should be happy anybody used your picture for anything other than target practice," I muttered, eager to escape that room and that house.

"I have a bone to pick with your publication."

"Yeah? You oughtta try working there. You'll get the whole skeleton."

"Oh, magazines are over. Zines are it," she said with an absurd certainty.

I realized the queen was attempting humor. Her outfit was attempting something, I wasn't sure what, a sort of white Uhuru on warp lag.

"Yes, I know dear, but zines don't pay the rent." And they break your heart.

"Zines are the pulse of this community. Your magazine is just an invasion."

"I think it covers the community quite well."

"It's never been near my ass!"

I scooted off the bed. "I don't recall it being on the map."

On the way downstairs, three men divulged their distinction from the ravey clubby crowd with a single sentence fragment that caught my ear.

"So, it's drinks at seven-thirty, dinner at eight."

Fabulous, I thought. Ferns and Shih-Tzus. I'm there. Snots.

I decided on one last desperate glance back, but saw Griffin nowhere. Who else might show up? The boy who beat me up in junior high school?

But there he was, standing by my bike. Griffin must have seen me try to escape, and stood by the bike, waiting, recognizing it.

I said nothing, but walked around him and busied myself with getting the bike unlocked and my helmet on.

"You just keep on pretending that everyone's expendable."

I said nothing. My keys were lost somewhere in a hole in my pocket. I panicked a moment, and stared at him, then found them down under the lining, and stuck the key in the ignition.

"It seems to you the thing to do would be to isolate the winner," he said.

It was then that I got it. His way of saying these words, out of joint, yet so appropriate. It chilled me that I knew what to say. "Everything's done under the sun," I replied with a false air of finality. I straddled the bike and gunned the gas, then pulled off the sidewalk and shouted out, "And I believe at heart everyone's a killer."

I rode around for a long time, not going home. I even rode up to Bernal Heights, just to prove that I could do it without caring if he was there, but all the while knowing I could go there because I knew he wasn't. Besides, he'd moved, I heard. I was a bit relieved not to know where.

If I had known, would I have skulked about the entrance to his home? Spying on his youth, his joy, his recklessness? He was going to be twenty-six soon. In her stage show, Eartha Kitt asks a waiter, who brings her a glass of water, how old he is. "Twenty-six," he says.

"Twenty-six? Twenty-six?" she cries, incredulous. "Twenty-six is a ridiculous age to be. Don't you know that nobody is twenty-six anymore?"

I wanted Griffin to be like that boy, be forced to drink, or suffer, or cry until he felt sixty-six. I wanted him to feel the heartache I felt, make his little addle-brained heart know what I went through. But I knew that he would be in the arms of another, and grinning the same grin he gave me, and maybe even trying a few positions or twists in sex that he explored with me, his new love thinking how unique and captivating was this man called Griffin.

What would I say if I could?

As I stopped at the intersection of Noe and Market, a Muni train passed. The rumbling cocoon's antenna ignited sparks on the cables above.

I looked down to see where they might fall. Spray-painted on the sidewalk, the word I thought might be some train conductor instruction: "DISENGAGE."

I parked in the Safeway, remembering to buy more of something for the long night at home. The Safeway's lights scared me, though, so I crossed the street to the liquor store.

At the corner a guy on the sidewalk was selling paperback books, a toaster and some junk. Laid out on a blanket among the stuff was a copy of DOGZ, with Griffin, perpetually catching a Frisbee.

I bought it, stood on the corner looking at it, then placed it in a garbage can. I just wanted to get it out of anybody's sight.

25

After my nurse practitioner declared a clean bill of health, I worked very hard at forgetting him, in Buena Vista Park at dusk, at The Cock Factory until dawn. That should have counted for points. It didn't work, but I at least had enjoyable sex with guys who didn't mean anything more to me than the moments of pleasure. I could play the loved one for a change. I could be the one remembered with longing.

But I couldn't shake the moments where I truly loved him. When we'd picked out earrings at Piedmont for the drag party, I had said I had to get clip-ons, since the piercing on my left lobe was unusable, since it had healed.

"No, it isn't," Griffin had said convincingly, and without hesitating, took an earring and popped it into my long-closed hole, freeing me to wear hoops on both sides. I never forgot the sound of that tiny rip in my skin, that moment of turning an old scar into something new.

Like I said, I am not of moneyed means. Too poor to buy new tapes, yet I always found the money to rent another video.

I began a surreptitious taping over of my porno, covering it with Visconti, Wenders, gay films, anything but sex. About sex, yes, but sex itself had become useless, a memory of an old man.

I taped over these burned in jackoff memories, hoping to turn back to actual live men.

Of course I failed, and lost a good collection of X while gaining some culture in the process. I turned to my magazines, and my words. Words work the imagination. You deserve your hardon when you read to get it.

Fiend couldn't have had a better name. Short-lived, junky, industrial, tattooed and basically non-clone queers inhabited the place, and the music and atmosphere were nothing like the usual gay stuff. So I went.

I'd gone there a few times, but seen him there too often to return. The last time could have ended up like one of those corny romances where the ex-lovers get in a brawl and end up kissing on the floor after tiring of punches.

But I couldn't even get to the fighting words stage.

I felt a quiver in my gut as Griffin sidled up to me, our mutual drag queen friend Primateen Miss chatting away with Griffin, as if I had never tearfully confessed my agony to her at losing him.

It was before Valentine's Day and P. Miss had painted little black hearts all over her face. She wore a tight gogo skirt in a pattern swiped from the walls of *Laugh-In*.

Griffin was flirting with her, but I saw him leering over her shoulder. I knew Griffin was using the queen to eventually get to me. He wouldn't win that, but he would win the silent turf fight. All Griffin's friends were there. I didn't want to imagine how many guys in that room Griffin had fucked, so I walked out, muttering shoulda said quips the whole walk home.

When I dreamed about him, the scenes were inevitably about barriers, and loss, distances. Walls, or in one case, a boat, all worked to separate me from him.

One night though, we were in a room filled with people and I said some words to him, casual, over a glass of something, that made him come with me.

I woke up too soon to see what would have happened. The magic words were lost when I tossed in bed, half awake, my blood shifting to the other side of my brain, erasing the memory like an Etch-a-Sketch.

26

I'd been doing pretty okay for a while, just remembering moments, sorting, disposing as I handed over the reins at work while faxing my resume to potential employers back in New York. Thinking of Griffin in that light made me wistful, but it had been too many months for me to continue in my misery, as much as I enjoyed the pose.

Until Bobbie Bubble had another bonfire. They were always fun, with cute boys and a few goth dykes and dragsters all out on Ocean Beach at night. People kept showing up, running off to dance in the sand, pass beer bottles, wine bottles, cigarettes, munchies, pot.

We huddled around the fire, watching the flood of flames as Bobbie tossed another crate on the fire, our eyes hypnotized under the glow of beer, wine or what have you.

I'd come with Denton and Vic, the loving couple, Harlan, and Curt Fenton, who'd blown into town from the East like the whirling gust of boyish energy he had, despite turning forty.

Denton and Vic gave us a ride. We packed into their car, Curt laid out over my lap and Harlan's, each of us toying with him, tickling him, grabbing his crotch, knowing our teasing would amount to nothing. Curt was the consummate flirt, always hinting of the possible.

As a dozen or so other queer folk told stories and laughed, drank beer and smoked dope, we huddled together, Harlan next to me, Curt on his side. I crept my hand under Harlan's sweat shirt, gradually easing it up his muscled belly. The warm folds were like waves locked in muscle. I tried to tell him that jokingly, like if it were a bad pun, he shouldn't be insulted. I felt Curt's hand on my shoulder, and wanted to kiss them both, but we were half shivering, our backs to the purple black roaring ocean, and half burning, our faces glowing and chafed from the sparks and flames.

I was determined to enjoy the evening, maybe hit on Curt one last time, but the winds blew up, some sparks flew, and the bonfire suddenly jumped in flames.

Griffin walked up into the sparks.

We avoided each other, sure, and I preened with my comfort, being surrounded by these two handsome men whom I craved endlessly.

But not like Griffin, whose only flaw was that he had said yes.

We skirted around each other as the group diminished, reduced to standing as Bobbie took one after another crate, forcing folks to stand or huddle in the sand. I chose to stand, and as Griffin edged closer occasionally, I found it suddenly necessary to lean close to Harlan, who also saw Griffin, or Curt, who knew nothing. He was too wrapped up in himself and his passions to notice the fallout of others. But then he too saw Griffin, who had sidled up to Bobbie, and tossed a glance my way. I stood between my friends, like unknowing bodyguards.

Protect me from what I want.

Curt was yammering about some queen he went home with, only to find out he was a total flake, but that he said something about some night where Saturn was in zero, or completion, or some astro stuff. It sounded groovy coming from him, and I feigned interest, when all I really wanted was to tell him to shut up and kiss me.

"Who's that?" Curt naively asked, nodding his head toward Griffin.

Harlan and I exchanged looks, then nodded back and forth, a silent game of hot potato.

"Don't get started," Harlan muttered.

"Don't," I replied.

"C'mon," I said to Curt. "Let's go look at the ocean." We rose and walked out into the darkness, where I heard a voice, his voice, Griffin, say, "Have a good drown!"

"What did he say?"

"I didn't hear a thing."

The waves grew louder, and the fire became a small light behind us. Curt rambled on about some boy, so I knew this wouldn't be the right time to try and plant a kiss on him, now that the whole beach was his. Griffin had a way of doing that, owning a place as soon as he'd made his territorial pissing, so to speak.

We were shivering, so Curt and I raced back, then only stopped at the bonfire long enough to round up Denton and Vic for the ride home. They were a couple, and were eager to get home and comfortable. Couples do that, I'm told.

Piled into the back seat, Harlan lying across our laps, Curt and I nodded heads close. I smelled him, noticed the little hairs along his temple that led to his closely cropped auburn scalp.

His strong Roman profile once caused me to blurt a poem to him about being a "horsy Adonis."

I could have sat nestled in the back seat of that car for hours, on into the night, but we rode into the Castro, parked, and ended up spilled out and squeezed into The Detour.

"I gotta take a piss. Come with me." Curt led me back though the cramped, sullen men amid the pulsing hateful techno beat and glare of pinball machines. Where was Catherine Deneuve, I always wondered as I passed the chain link fence.

Curt whipped out his penis, as did I, and we giggled. "Cross streams," he blurted, and we did, our piss mingling in the red-glowing trough. I remembered that the last time I'd seen his dick was in someone's bathroom at a party, pissing together then as well, and even then I couldn't understand. Was he being blatant? Was this how he flirted, showing his water sports tastes? Or was he just teasing? That seemed more like it. I nearly leaned over and gulped some of his piss down, but I didn't know how far he would go.

"I love pee. I could play with it all the time," he said.

"I'm happy to know that, Curt," I said, secretly thrilled. "I like it, too. But not in public." Liar.

I felt a sudden urge to kiss Curt again, to grab his cock and demand the sex I always wanted, the sex I damn near begged for often enough with him. But something, perhaps the sighting of Griffin, kept me down, and I finished whizzing, buttoned up, and returned back out with him. Hadn't I shown enough interest? Hadn't I fawned over him all night, without so much as a grope of lust? "You could piss all night if you come home with me," I wanted to say.

Flippant as ever, though, Curt turned away to chat up a bartender as we returned to the thudding crush of awkward men. Did he offer a drink? Even a word? No, he was off.

"I was in love with you for way too long," I said to his back. "Two weeks, maybe."

I didn't even bother to find the boyfriends, or Harlan, who undoubtedly had latched onto some gym bunny he'd hit on before. Happy hunting, gents, I said, as I picked up a copy of the magazine, scanned the masthead to be assured that I was no longer a part of that world, and walked home.

I resolved not to merely pound my pud in a tribute to the men who spurned me. How many? No, it was a night to dive in. My Saturn was in zero.

"It isn't like someone you know, someone who's brought you soup when you're sick couldn't also kiss your butt," I blurted as I combed my hair in the bathroom.

"It isn't like someone you've been arrested with doesn't merit a blow job or a toss once, at least," I thought as I gargled, but didn't brush my teeth.

"God forbid you should fuck someone you know," I seethed as I tossed my sneakers and laced my Doc Martins.

"If that's how you like it," I said to my imagined Curt, as I grabbed my helmet and headed out the door, "pretend we never met."

235-? (Lost count)

It was a good night for bold decisions. I slipped past zombie intersections all the way down into the breast of SoMa, not stopping until I passed the mural of muscled working men next door to The Cock Factory. I was gonna suck and get blown until I couldn't even remember their names.

Good thing trusty old Anders was sitting pretty atop the barber chair. Although we'd buddy-sucked and jerked off in a few tight places before, I just decided to pull an act to please to crowd, who could have just come from the Detour. It might as well have been the Detox. It might as well have been anywhere, the craven, hollow-eyed look so similar in all the men, except the beauties that had little adulatory cruisers following them around, awaiting a parking spot so they could see some pec boy unleash his weenie. I wouldn't have that. I licked Ander's boots to begin with.

I had to piss away the beer I had with Curt, so I retreated to the john and rubbed the balding head of a gent who lapped it up, just as I had done with Griffin, as I would have done with Curt, in the Detox, or anywhere, if he asked. But he didn't ask. This guy at my knees didn't have to, and I patted his head and blurted a "Thanks," as I dribbled a bit of piss on his 'stache.

Unable to crush out the thoughts of Griffin, Harlan or Curt, I took pleasure in the last sordid mix of men. The guy slathering away below me had short hair, a cut-off flannel shirt, and a long strong nose. In that light, it was close enough. I could have been getting blown by Curt.

That wasn't enough. Another came up as I thought I might be done for the night, a tall cubby bear of a guy, with a sweet, confused face, a flat nose and a huge thick cock, about the girth I always imagined Harlan's to be, and clean, fresh, like he'd just shown up. Slobbering down on that would have been enough, what with faux-Curt going to town on my cock, my hands brushing through his buzz cut, but then another hand crept to my butt, and damn if he didn't poke into my ass just the way Griffin did when he was itching for a fuck.

I shot on Curt's head and all over anything nearby. Sweaty, drenched in sex smells, I almost left, but the big-dicked one wanted to hug, and then kiss, and then come, and I liked that more than anything else, of course, that crunching hug. He popped three of my vertebrae and gave me a big smooch, wet and sloppy, and he wouldn't let go, and I knew why when I felt his ejaculate coat my belly.

The damp spots in my jeans cooled against my thighs as I rode home, me singing softly to the music in my head: "Making love with somebody exactly like you, and you can't do a thing....to stop me."

"A lover can be a best friend,
a piece of furniture, or an eternity."

– Sam D'Allesandro,
"Electrical Type of Thing"

27

Starving after a ride down to Santa Cruz (Bagged a surfer. Sorry, that'll have to be another time), I rode Rose into the Castro for a quick sandwich. I felt energized and relaxed, as if I had gained re-entry. Men noticed me, my buzzed hair, my windburned face, the exhilaration still glowing under my skin.

I decided to do a little window shopping, stopped in A Different Light and splurged on a few books, checked to make sure my zines were sold out, then headed down the street to the new video store, since I heard they had some bootleg copies of *Wild Wild West* episodes.

They were out, of course, but there were a few gay films I wanted to watch. Then of course, my groin led me to the rows of porno tapes, each one more boring than the other. Cascade of cocks, smooth muscle bodies, all looking damn near the same.

I moved down the special interest porn section, and my heart thudded.

It was Griffin, in a box.

I paid four dollars, trying to keep my hand steady, nearly quivering. Finally, I was going to see it. I was going to have him on tape, contained, the way I wanted all along.

I nearly spun out on the way home, but finally I got the tape out, "Initiation Rites," starring Matt Wolf. A ridiculously appropriate porn name. On the label, the text said the performers were "broken by trained personnel."

It was one of those inane, tie-em-up and torture tapes. Not a boner in sight. Just an amazing array of ropes and clamps and whips and racks.

He looked...well, ridiculous.

Clamps, tit torture, shaving, all the while he was tied up, shackled and generally abused. I know that thousands of men, and women, of all sexual orientations find pleasure in bondage and SM, as have I, but watching it, without the feel of it, either receiving or giving, is often silly. It has no bearing on the voyeur.

Bondage and SM, unlike plain old sex, has less thrill for the watcher. You can't feel the heat of the crop smacking on your butt. You can't feel the surge of power as the cuffs click your slave into position.

I wanted that, the tension, the passion, the trust, and no video could hold that, or record it, or retrieve it between Griffin and I. That was gone, rinsed away, sweat down a drain.

His butt, the white valentine, flexing, being spanked and slapped by a mysterious man in jeans, gave me a hot rush, not of desire, but revenge. It made me happy to see him enjoying himself, and that he was paid for it, and that with the tape he got to spread his slutty reputation around with obvious evidence.

But what gave me a darker pleasure was a sadism unlike the usual, not one of giving pleasure through pain, but knowing he was genuinely hurting, that every slap and pinch and wrenching of his balls and flesh matched every tear, every night I spent trying to beat off thinking about him, only to end up limp in despair.

Every whack of pain that made him shout matched every distracted lonely thought that kept me home, afraid to start anything with another man, even after the train wreck of orgies and sex clubs from the previous year.

Every burn of his skin with wax dripped for my every tear. He was suffering, and I loved it. My copy hasn't worn out yet.

Other than that, I never saw him again. It was as if he vanished from San Francisco before I did.

I like to think that he is the demon he resembled, and had merely shifted his shape to hide from the hearts he'd damaged, a self-protecting morph-like device to guard him from vengeful lovers like me. Who knows how many?

He's got a new name now, maybe, a new face, different hair, and new lovers to crush with his wicked smile, the smile of a thief, and I long for him to return to the scene of his crime.

28

A woman came up to me at a nightclub; Rump, Sleaze, whatever. I didn't recognize her.

"You know, you really fucked up. He liked you a lot."

"Liked?"

"Yeah. What's wrong with that?"

"You are..?"

"His roommate...for a time."

I recognized her from the party, and that morning. Donna. But her hair was darker. She was just kind of plain, and beautiful...healed.

"You know, we dated for a while," she said.

I didn't turn toward her, but that didn't help hide my shock. Of course, all those people, every one of them, under his spell, strung along. Maybe not sexually, maybe very sexually, maybe he just compartmentalized them all so swiftly that we never noticed.

"He really liked you," she said again.

"Like that means I could have stayed with him?"

"Maybe."

"See, that's just it, the maybe. Maybe we'll be together tonight."

He coughed. "Maybe I'll have wild sex with you in some bizarre place, maybe we'll cozy up to a bowl of popcorn, maybe we'll get in a brawl in a hustler bar."

I shook my head, shaking it from me like heavy rain. She sipped her drink and waited.

"I was in love with him and he nearly drove me mad. What we could have had exploded. I have a life now. My life."

"What, remembering him? Recovering from him?"

"Maybe."

"If you'd given yourself to him, you could have known complete happiness."

"Like you?"

"This isn't about me. It's about you and him. You could have been his, forever."

"Fitted with collar and chain?" I brushed her off, furious that she could unearth all those raw emotions after so long. And yet I felt stronger, as if the last layers of his hold on me fell off in that bar.

Further up the coast, Kurt Cobain's decaying body would be found in a pool of brain and blood.

Teenagers in flannel would huddle around candles and pictures of the dead grunge king.

I would have mourned, but I had an anniversary. Easter Sunday.

I rode to the shore on my new bike, which I call Bud (Rose never quite recovered from the spinout). I watched surfers down at Ocean Beach dance in the waves. Moving up the hill at the Seal Rocks, I parked Bud in the lot and walked along the path to above Land's End. Looking down, I saw people dotting the cliff-scape, and below, the myriad paths of mystery and pleasure, the cruising ground.

The easiest path is always the least challenging, so I took a smaller trail that got steep by the outlet of an underground spring. I tromped down to ground level, where a large clearing under the arc of a huge cedar showed three men, standing, a nervous triangle, indecisive. Who would move first?

I walked right up into it, disrupting the tension, and checked each one out. None too exciting. A small underbrush trail called me. I swooped under a thick limb, and jumped up just in time to avert the grope of a potbellied guy with pink shorts.

"How ya doin'?" he said.

"Fine."

"You're a real monkey." I was out of his reach. "Can I suck yer dick?"

"No, thanks, I'm not up for that now."

I stood higher and saw a muscular shirtless guy, his pecs dusted in blond hairs, smiling at me. He was coy. I nudged him to come to me. He stood, smiling, like, I'm worth you coming to me. But then I figured he was doing the lure thing, getting off more on being wanted than letting anyone have it.

I did some of that too, loping down vine and tree-covered paths, crouching to clutch my dick under my shorts while listening to another tiny brook trickle. Bits of sun glinted through spiderwebs and leaves. I stood and jacked my cock slowly, growing stiff as a guy approached. As he faced me, I flopped my cock back in my jams, just at the last moment. Tease.

After a little nude rock designing down at the beach, I got wet (It's hard to swim in such rocky waters, but the tingle of walking back to your clothes while all eyes watch is worth it), then dressed and walked back up to a high spot, somewhere with a great view.

Jutting out from Land's End like a widow's walk for the city, the plateau wasn't the highest, but it was beautiful and somewhat private. A bit of cruising went on between a few guys, but I got a craving for view over spew.

Dead spears of broken limbs jutted from the tree's base like a stairway. I climbed, found a comfy joint between limbs, parked my ass on the hard root of a major limb, and pulled off my shirt, hanging my backpack on a nearby limb. I was fifteen feet up in a huge cedar, and the ocean was a big blue plate.

It was funny watching the traffic below, guys darting in and out of shrubs, others standing, lookout, posing. Some could see me from afar, none from below. I hovered like a panther, watching the prey, sorting, lording.

On a bank about a hundred yards away, a man appeared, sporting cliché garb that nonetheless caught my eye. Red sleeveless flannel shirt, jams, and hiking boots. Complete.

He seemed rather handsome from that distance, although the air made everyone sort of glow. He saw me and leaned against a waist high rock, pushing his hips out and cupping his hand over his eyes to see me.

I dug my hands into my pants, the sun warming my torso. I lay my book aside and let it get good and stiff before flopping out with it, slowly pumping, whapping it against my belly.

He seemed to like the show, but disappeared after some gaggle of hets dundered through. I'd hidden my dick and watched them pass under me seeking escape. They'd tread into strange territory, and I couldn't resist the urge to utter a low growl.

I watched more men pop in and out, and the boats on the water, matchstick kites.

The man soon appeared, standing below, grinning up at me.

"Seems you've got the best parking spot."

"There's room for one more."

He was up in about four seconds.

"Wow." He looked at the view, and then at me, and I think both of us were rather impressed.

He said I had a handsome face. It was red from the sun. He had a heavy shadow of a beard. Panther eyes. Those boots. Total Timberland. I believed him. My hair cut short as a marine, my face free of hair, I felt clean of the previous year, and for once, finally, I felt handsome again.

We talked of religion, art, dish, high school crushes. Hell, I don't know how it was we darted around so, something that always turns me on, the ability to make great conversation.

"Have you ever jacked off up here?" he said.

"No."

"'Fraid of fallin' off?"

"No, just... I just feel like a lazy cat who's just had his dinner walk up to him."

"Well, I gotta pee." He gripped one leg against a thicker trunk, and unzipped his shorts, fished his cock out, and let go down, far down, to the ground. I held out my hand, as if before a fountain, and cupped some of it, then slathered it over my belly.

He grinned, sly. "Nature's sunblock," he said, finishing off and waggling his penis, which had grown half-hard.

I liked that he didn't zip up, just left it there, peeking out, as he sat down next to me.

We moved slowly, talked softer, and became invisible again. Guys passed below, unseeing, or if they did, a mere nod of appreciation or furtive glance, and all we had to do was look down to shoo them away.

Hands on thighs, our cocks were out, red and cheerful to feel the brisk air. The branches splayed out where we sat, like intwined hammocks of wood. His thighs occasionally quivered as he readjusted himself, his legs clutching a large trunk.

Our bellies and legs got some of the warm breeze by the time our pants were down enough to let out our balls and cocks, and between sucking slurps on each other's cock, we glanced up to watch the sun bleed through the pine branches.

I can't recall which was my favorite moment; my dick spitting my sperm over his beard-stubbled face as he hovered over it, my gaze distracted by the rusted disc descending at that moment, or, after bringing him up to witness the sunset, licking the come off him, scooping it out of the cleft in his chin while he giggled, trying to hold a Mount Rushmore pose.

I liked the way he shoved his hips forward, so that when he came, the loops of sperm laced the tree trunk. I rubbed it into the bark, then brought my hand to my hair, digging it in, nature's hair gel.

All indecision about what I was, and how I lived, faded away. I knew then how I needed open air, just to remind me that I was once an animal. It was like that episode of *Northern Exposure* where, once a year, in the middle of winter, all the straight guys got to run naked through the streets. Except I could do it whenever I wanted.

It was then that I had a clearer view of why I enjoyed Griffin's daring, and how he had brought it out in me. The idea of public sex was not the thrill of getting caught, or its potential.

Of course, the intensity of having someone barge in on your mountain top orgasm mid-spurt, and the shock of that, was a neat idea. Who could be watching? A hapless straight couple? A lanky park ranger?

But no, that wasn't it. Too bawdy. I wanted to be with others who wanted to see and be seen. I wanted a naked man on every outcrop and rock platform to be naked and hard and enjoying himself too.

It was doing it in a beautiful public spot and doing the most appropriate thing to do at such a beautiful moment; claim the space as your own, the public land as yours, and enjoy it fully.

Adding sex, mindful to others and worshipful to the outdoor gods and faery under-the-leaf things, was not only fun, but verged on holy.

Take the gun turrets. Hundreds of them dug into hillsides all over. How many soldiers spent long, boring nights jacking off or screwing or sucking in these scenic perches, with only each other for entertainment? We were re-living those actions, in those places, although sometimes they might be covered in ivy, or littered by beer cans. That just made it better.

The decay, the sense of moments so far gone they have to come around again, and you're driven, on some bike ride night, or broad sunny day, to a flat and good plain atop a hillside, and you just have to get your hands on some guy's cock, with your pants down to your ankles and freighters going by.

The freedom to talk and lick the man was due, in part, by the beauty of our surroundings, but also, inside, I knew I'd changed. I wasn't a dog anymore.

29

I figured out the cologne he used. I got some, but not on purpose. It was after a huge overblown AIDS benefit at the Fashion Center. The going away gift bags had samples. I tried some when I got home with my date, the tree guy. His name's...oh, fuck you, I'm not telling.

Each of us drunk on too much champagne and not enough food, our tuxes ended up tossed into a pile in the hall after I'd knelt and sucked his dick, pale, jutting from the black suit, a velvet spear, stark.

Sure, he was handsome, and his cock tickled me in the right places, but after the first round, I walked to the kitchen where we'd dropped the bags and dabbed a bit of the cologne on my neck.

It was like bottled Griffin.

I went back to my tree guy, and he'd peeled off everything but paisley silk boxers, his cock still jutting up, awaiting some coat to hang on it, some ass to envelope it, hide its stark urgency.

"Man, you never let me fuck you before. What's with you?"

I'm not sure if he smelled it, or just thought it was a joke, but I pumped the come out of him soon enough, and he liked it, enough to come back for more, sometimes.

He's efficient, handsome. We've got a lot in common. But he hasn't got what I lost. There's no wondering where, or when or in what wild position we'll do it again. He's stable, like a thick post, and I guess I'll wrap my strap around it for a while, but, I'll be honest, he's a little boring. Nice.

It's nothing like what I had, and it won't last. He's not worthy staying for. He still doesn't know why I won't go out in public with him. I'd love to, but I know out there the talons of the sour are ready to shred anything so fragile as love, or its resemblance.

I don't know what sense of community one is supposed to get from the life here. I do know that the air of coolness, the freedom, is merely a mask for those too afraid, or empty, to feel, to really love another. I see their hesitance, hear the distance in conversation. I tell no one of this affair.

A mere sentence, a mere phrase referring to it, and I see the eyes glaze over, the head tilting a moment, then scan their fog-soaked brains for another topic, quick. Then, in soft murmurs, "He's the one who used to date..."

Sometimes I'd make out a figure walking down the street with the same bouncing slouch, the same cropped hair, the same clothes.

But then I see there is no glow under the glare, no sly grin that promises anything and gives everything. There is no sliver under the silver. It is as if, having done with him, he no longer exists.

I don't travel the path where I might find him. Maybe he just disappeared. No one knows where he is. Even with that comfort of his apparent move, or death, or displacement - perhaps he's ensconced into the home and arms of a man who keeps him at home, with only a brief run through the park after work for a spot of outdoor time - I know I'll see him again.

And I fear that. I fear my reaction more than anything. I fear my willingness to get on all fours and beg him, once more, right there on the pavement.

Instead, I rode through my last days there, before leaving for good.

You won't see me on the path of men. I will be off the curb, astride my bike, hidden under my helmet's guise, recognizable only to those who may have shared the rumble of my wheels. I work alone, live alone, and find no lovers to compare. The fog envelops in its silence, turning the night sky a jaundiced glowing yellow, the pallor of night people. The fog comes, and I enter its silent embrace.

Tom Bacchus is the author lots of stories, originally published in lots of magazines and anthologies, including the paperback editions of *Bone*, *Rahm* and *Poke,* the science fiction sex satire *Q-FAQ*, and *Doin' the Town*, a naughty nautical novella.

Enjoy his NSFW ramblings and naughty stuff at:

http://tombacchus.blogspot.com/

https://twitter.com/Tom_Bacchus

https://www.goodreads.com/author/show/757696.Tom_Bacchus

https://tombacchus.reblogme.com/

www.ingramcontent.com/pod-product-compliance
Lightning Source LLC
LaVergne TN
LVHW021759060526
838201LV00058B/3168